SECRET BEYOND THE MOUNTAINS

By Rita Ritchie

THE YEAR OF THE HORSE
THE GOLDEN HAWKS OF GENGHIS KHAN
THE ENEMY AT THE GATE
SECRET BEYOND THE MOUNTAINS

RITA RITCHIE

Secret Beyond the Mountains

E. P. DUTTON & COMPANY, INC.
NEW YORK · 1960

LIBRARY OF CONGRESS CATALOG CARD NUMBER: 60-11862

To FRANK *and* ANNETTE KROHNE

CONTENTS

He galloped through the night, the chuffing of his horse and the clatter of hoofs constant in his ears. Ahead in the moonlight stretched the post road that had been pounded across the steppe by thousands of horses.

Far down on the horizon a cluster of orange dots glowed against the night's pinprick of stars. A post station! Taikal urged forward his rangy Mongol horse. Stretching its neck in a final burst of speed, his mount thundered down the earth-packed road.

Freeing one hand from the reins, Taikal felt for the leather bags of cooked rice and milk tied to his belt. His fingers touched the quiver on his right hip, the sword on his left. On his back he found lance and bow firmly bound, as was the copper tiger tablet on his leather armored chest. His metal helmet with its red crest was tightly strapped on. All was secure.

The post station was closer now. He could see in the torchlight the yurts which housed the men on duty, and beyond them the corral.

Taikal raised his horn and blew the signal.

Just two days ago Taikal had been in Karakorum. The city of Genghis Khan had been his home for the past year, ever since Onantu, Taikal's father, had died a valiant death in the Cathayan wars. Genghis Khan had rewarded his hero through the son, summoning Taikal from his northern home so that he might be enrolled in the cadet officers' school.

Although Karakorum was the greatest ordu in the empire, its people lived in the familiar yurt, the domed-shaped dwelling of felt over a wicker framework. Nor did Taikal's clothes mark him as an outsider, for he wore the same deerskin shirt as did the others, the same sheepskin jacket, full-cut felt trousers, and leather or skin boots with upturned toes. Even the weapons, metal helmet, and lacquered leather armor he had been given were like those of the other cadets. Yet Taikal had found it hard to make friends. Most of the cadets in the school rebuffed his friendly overtures, for they were sons of officers while Taikal's father had served in the ranks. Of the others his age, only Yarkut had not taunted him for the direct, sometimes rough, manners Taikal had brought with him from the isolated ordu of his tribe. The two had become fast friends.

Taikal and Yarkut lived in the same yurt, one of several set aside for those boys whose homes were outside Karakorum. Together they drilled their horses, practiced their weapons, and worked on strategy problems under the critical eyes of the generals who were their instructors. They helped each other with the tasks the scholars assigned them in writing, geography, and languages.

"I will give you yet another study," promised Yarkut. "I have been in Karakorum long enough to learn ways different from those of my home in the east. Now I will smooth your manners and trim your blunt tongue."

And so, with Yarkut's help, Taikal slowly had begun to shed his clumsy ways. By spring the cruel teasing had disappeared. Yet new friendships had been hindered by the beating of war drums.

"Word has come that Gutchluk, the khan of Kara Khitai,

has invaded our western border," Yarkut told Taikal one evening. "Chepe Noyon said that tomorrow he will select the cadets who are to ride into battle with the army. Perhaps we can go together, Taikal!"

But Taikal's name was not on the list the general read out the next day, though all cadets his age were assigned. Seeking him out, Taikal found Chepe Noyon with Soo, the crossbowman. Boldly he asked if a mistake had not been made.

"No, lad," Chepe said. "I have not forgotten you. But I think it best if you remain in Karakorum with the younger cadets." He gestured Taikal's protest aside. "Yes, I know you are as skilled with weapons as the others your age. But they have ridden into battle beside their fathers, and so warfare is not new to them."

"But I rode beside my father, too!"

"Tribal skirmishes!" Chepe exclaimed. "Border protection! A matter of stolen horses, or trespassing on grazing grounds."

"The arrows were none the less real," Taikal said.

Chepe roared with laughter. "A good wit and a brave heart! Soo, what would you say to this lad?"

"I say leave him here with me," the crossbowman answered. "I will try him in the summer maneuvers, and if he does well I will send him to the hunt at war's end."

"Agreed!" Chepe Noyon clapped Taikal on the shoulder. "Work hard, Taikal, and if you join the hunt I will have you ride beside me."

Taikal was cheered by the general's promise, for Chepe Noyon was the most popular officer among the cadets. His good humor and willingness to take a jest made them all work hard to meet his high standards.

Yet it was with a heavy heart that Taikal watched the

great army move out of Karakorum, led by Genghis Khan's standard of nine white yak tails and carved eagle. Behind the Khan the generals trotted by—Bayan, Subotai, and Chepe Noyon, their white horsetail crests swinging with the rhythm of their mounts' hoofs, their armor gleaming in the sun. The mass of men and officers followed. Here and there among them a helmet bearing a red crest marked a cadet officer. Each cadet would ride beside his father or an assigned officer. More troops would join the army as it moved westward, for messengers had been sent out with the call to arms.

Farewells were shouted between the warriors and those staying behind. "May the Blue Sky keep you safe!" from mothers and wives was answered with the traditional, "Keep well the yurt!"

Taikal rode back to his own yurt after the army had entered the great plain surrounding the city. The dwelling of felt was deserted but for two or three younger boys. Taikal had hardly entered through the low doorway when someone outside called his name.

Soo sat on his horse, two crossbows and a wicker shield strapped to the cantle. "It is a fine time for crossbow practice today, Taikal."

"But this is a free day," Taikal protested.

"If you do not work hard, I can not send you to join the hunt this fall," Soo replied.

"A hunt is hardly a battle," Taikal grumbled.

Soo leaned forward. "You have never seen a hunt such as Genghis Khan holds at the end of summer. The cadets are given actual command, and the wild charges of beasts which must be driven but not killed will try courage and cleverness to the utmost. Truly, the hunt will give you more experience than dozens of mock battles here in school. Now do you think the goal worthy of crossbow practice?"

Taikal ran for his horse.

He worked and studied hard through the long hot days of summer. During the month of maneuvers Soo had organized for mock battles, Taikal forgot it was a game and he warred earnestly. At night in the almost empty yurt he practiced brush strokes and memorized maps by the light of a flickering sheep-fat lamp.

And then one day a messenger galloped in to Karakorum, the copper tiger tablet on his chest and his horse flecked with foam. Later Soo called Taikal to him.

"The war has come to an end for this summer," Soo told him. "The great hunt will begin soon."

"Is it not early for breaking off the engagement?" asked Taikal. "It is not yet harvest time."

Soo nodded gravely. "That is true, yet Gutchluk has sent the Khan word that he fears the early rains his astrologers have foreseen. The Khan has accepted the truce, for matters have not gone well in the field these last weeks." Then he smiled. "You are lucky to have less time for waiting, Taikal. Now here is a task for you; supplies must be sent to the army, and I wish you to draw up plans for the caravan."

For the next few days Taikal's brain was whirling with quantities and supply items. Trail rations, winter clothing, and the blunt weapons of the hunt were taken from the great earthen storehouses and packed for the long journey. Fresh meat for the troops would come from the sheep and yaks sent directly from the westernmost tribes. Taikal sent off the supplies in carts drawn by camels and in wagons pulled by the long-haired, great horned yaks. Some merchants and entertainers went with the caravan, for the warriors would provide a brisk trade during the hunt.

Two hours later, fully armed, Taikal galloped into the hills along the post road, carrying a sealed report from Soo to Genghis Khan. At his chest gleamed the messenger's copper tiger tablet, and a horn swung from his neck. He would change mounts every fifty miles, riding three horses in a day and a night. There would be no rest, no dismounting to cook a meal. The pounding of hoofs echoed the singing of his heart. He was not to ride with a mere captain or commander, but with a general, with Chepe Noyon!

For two days Taikal galloped on. At night the moon and stars lighted his way, and each post horse strained its hardened muscles as Taikal left the grassy steppe and entered the Gobi Desert.

The flat stretches of the Gobi gradually rumpled into hills, the barren ground supporting larger patches of vegetation as he neared the western border. Taikal forded icy streams born in distant mountains, slipping from the saddle and holding his mount's tail as the horse swam across. He wound up into the jagged mountains of the Altai range, struggling through snowdrifts in the higher passes. He threaded through vast dark forests of pine and beech, then finally left the Altai behind.

When hunger and thirst arose during his long ride, a reach under the saddle for a bit of the dried meat softening there and the loosening of a sack of milk or a bag of rice was his meal. When fatigue swept over him, he braced himself in the saddle and dozed as he had been accustomed to do since childhood.

Now ahead in the moonlight lay the last post station on the western road. His horse drummed down the track. By the light of the many torches Taikal saw a warrior start galloping away from the post, leading a fresh mount.

Taikal swept past the station, the torches only a blur, the shouted greetings lost in the thunder of hoofs. The soldier ahead was holding the horses down to let Taikal come up. Taikal edged his horse close to the new mount, galloping side by side. He kicked his feet out of the stirrups, then leaned over and grasped the pommel of the empty saddle, swinging himself on to the new horse. The warrior threw him the reins. Taikal's new horse put on a burst of speed, storming down the post road and leaving the warrior and the old mount behind.

Dawn found the road at an end. Following Soo's directions, Taikal galloped across a great plain, tearing off a bit of meat from the slab that had been put beneath the saddle at the post station.

Soon he passed the western boundary of Genghis Khan's empire. By noon he found an old campsite and slowed his horse to circle the area. Picking up the army's trail, he followed it, holding his horse down to conserve its strength. There would be no remounts until he had joined the Khan's forces. The route ran through steep wooded hills. Twice he had to cross rivers. Then, just as the sun was sinking, he topped a ridge. Before him the woods fell away, and on the plain below the army was encamped.

He moved down the slope, to be challenged and passed by sentries bristling with sharp weapons. Taikal rode down among the small trail yurts toward the great white yurt of Genghis Khan. Seeing the flash of a tiger tablet in the fading sunlight, a guard ran forward to take the scroll Taikal handed him.

Taikal trotted toward the herds to change his tired horse

for a fresh one while he searched for Yarkut. There he found Chepe Noyon carefully examining the hoof of his favorite mount. The general called a hearty greeting when he saw Taikal.

"So you have escaped the watchful eye of Soo! But when you ride with me you will discover that things were easier in Karakorum." The setting sun gleamed on the general's red lacquered breastplates, making the gold dragon painted there snarl and writhe across his chest. The full trousers tucked into his shiny black boots were bright with embroidery. Plainly he had put off his battle dress at the first opportunity in order to wear the resplendent costumes he favored. Chepe Noyon bore good-naturedly the jests his fine clothing often provoked.

"Soo said I would be given a command during the hunt," Taikal said. "What position will I hold?"

"First I will see how you manage a few scouting parties," Chepe answered. "Now I suppose you are looking for your friend Yarkut. He is in the regiment that was commanded by Jiemdad. But he can tell you little about the capture, since he was not among those taken prisoner." Chepe gave him directions.

Taikal made his way through the huge encampment until he found Yarkut before a small two-man trail yurt, patiently turning a chunk of mutton over a fire.

"Taikal!" Yarkut leaped up and seized his friend's hand in the hardened grip of the archer.

Clumsy with weariness, Taikal dismounted. He sniffed the roasting mutton hungrily.

Urging Taikal to eat, Yarkut unsaddled his mount and sent it off with a herder.

"Trail rations for three days and two nights," Taikal said,

as he crammed his mouth full of the juicy meat. "This is wonderful."

"Eat your fill," Yarkut said. "Our fresh meat will not last long, and we are short of trail rations, although the Khan has sent for supplies."

At the end of the meal Taikal yawned and rubbed his stinging eyes.

"Take my blanket and go to sleep," Yarkut said. "I will get another from the supply carts. The cadet who used to share the yurt with me was killed when Jiemdad was captured."

"Chepe Noyon said something about that." Taikal roused himself. "What happened?"

"Most of our regiment was surrounded and taken captive four weeks ago," Yarkut said. "My company managed to cut loose, but the rest were made prisoners. Then some days ago Bayan took in a force and rescued them. But Jiemdad, the commander, had been taken to Gu-Balik."

"That is the capital of Kara Khitai, is it not?" Taikal asked. "Gutchluk, the khan, stays there when he is not in the field against Khoresmia or us Mongols."

Yarkut nodded. "Soon after the regiment was rescued, Gutchluk sued for the winter's truce. We are badly undermanned, so we accepted. The Khan has not yet named a commander to take Jiemdad's place."

That night Taikal slept deeply. It was noon before he opened his eyes. He had hardly eaten when Chepe Noyon sent for him. They rode outside the yurts and carts of the camp, and then the general had Taikal show how well he performed with lance, bow and arrow, sword, crossbow, and snare.

As they were riding back, Chepe jerked his reins, making his horse prance. "Look, Taikal."

He pointed to the low hills westward. A lone horseman galloped toward the camp. "A Karakhitaian!"

"But if the sentries let him pass. . . ."

When the man rode closer, Taikal could see that he wore his bow around his neck in the display of submission. "A messenger from Gutchluk!" Taikal exclaimed.

"Return to the camp," Chepe ordered. "I will escort this man in." Chepe spurred his horse forward while Taikal reluctantly turned back to the camp. He told Yarkut the news, and they guessed wildly what message the Karakhitaian had brought.

Yarkut had gone off to collect their evening rations when one of the Khan's guards rode up to the trail yurt, leading a saddled horse. "If you are the cadet Taikal, I am to bring you to the yurt of the Khan."

Taikal dropped the bridle he had been mending for Yarkut. "I am the one you seek." He ducked into the low trail yurt and hurriedly strapped on helmet and breastplates. Then with a rag he furiously scrubbed a shine on his boots. Snatching up his weapons, he rejoined the guard.

Trotting through the camp, Taikal was glad he was coming before Genghis Khan as a young warrior. He had been in the Khan's presence only once before when he had come to Karakorum to receive the honor won him by his father Onantu. He must have looked then as he had felt—a lonely youth from the ordu of a far-off tribe. Now he sat his horse proudly in the arms and armor of a cadet officer.

They dismounted before the guards ranged in front of the Khan's large yurt. Taikal gave up his lance, sword and bow in accordance with custom.

Following his guide down the white horse-skin carpet inside the yurt, Taikal could not keep his eyes from the splendid silken hangings and the great variety of weapons on the walls. Most of the yurt was gloomy but for the sunlight slanting through the smoke hole. But the far end was ablaze with light from the huge brass bowls burning scented woods.

Here sat Genghis Khan on a carved and lacquered chair. The arrival of an enemy emissary had caused him to put off the simple soldier's garments he usually wore. Now with the flaming light flickering on highly polished plate armor, dancing along the gold embroidery of his trousers, and twining through the rich red of his long hair and beard, the conqueror was even more magnificent than Chepe Noyon in his own brilliant attire. The Khan's gray eyes were iron-hard with repressed anger as he studied the Karakhitaian kneeling before him.

On either side of Genghis Khan, sitting on silken cushions, ranged his scholars, generals, and other men privileged to attend the councils.

His guide paused to let Taikal approach the Khan. Taikal bowed deeply as Yarkut had often instructed him and uttered the customary greeting.

Genghis Khan gestured to the Karakhitaian who knelt to one side with a back stiff with insolence.

"This man has come from Gutchluk to parley for Jiemdad's ransom," the Khan told Taikal.

Taikal glanced swiftly at the men attending the council. Their faces were set with cold anger.

"The ransom is high indeed," the Khan continued. "We must retreat to Chensi Nor, losing territory it took most of the summer to win. We must also send gold, jewels, and other goods." He sent a piercing look at the Karakhitaian. "Gutch-luk would not pay a ransom such as this even for his son."

The Karakhitaian answered boldly. "My master bids me tell you to be comforted with only the loss of sheared wool now. For when the grass grows green in spring, he will come as a wolf upon your flock and scatter those he does not slay."

Genghis Khan gripped the arms of his throne until his knuckles turned white. "My warriors are as the sturdy oaks in the forest. If a boar comes among them, I must give him acorns to eat lest his greedy tusks chafe away the bark. But let Gutchluk know this: when the snows melt in spring, I will come with many arrows and I will slay the boar."

The Khan turned to Taikal. "You are to head the ransom train, Taikal. Take thirty men with you, but have them carry their weapons in a peaceful manner." He told Taikal of the time and place agreed upon. Then he turned once more to the arrogant Karakhitaian. "Study this youth well, so you may know him when he journeys to the meeting place. Your master will not take it kindly should you mistake Taikal's group for a raiding party."

Taikal turned to let the Karakhitaian see his face. The emissary's eyes traveled over his features, fixing them in his mind. Then he nodded. "I will not mistake him."

When the Khan dismissed him, Taikal bowed low, but his head was high and proud as he left the white yurt and reclaimed his weapons. Thirty men meant three squads, each with its lieutenant. And he, Taikal, would be their captain!

Later, during the evening meal, Yarkut congratulated Taikal on his good fortune. "This will surely make up for having missed the summer's battles, for none of us was given command."

"Perhaps Chepe Noyon persuaded the Khan to appoint me

to this task," Taikal replied. "He remembered my disappointment this spring." He shook his head. "Yet my mission is not a happy one, for no one wishes to treat with Karakhitaians."

That week it was a dispirited army which slowly marched back to the line set by the enemy. Only the Khan's promise to retake the territory the next summer kept up its hopes. Men were sent racing over the post road to bring from Karakorum the treasures demanded by Gutchluk. The army's best horses, all its remaining sheep, and those yaks not used for drawing carts were rounded up for the Karakhitaians. The Khan's troops would have to subsist on reduced trail rations until new herds were brought in.

Chepe Noyon helped Taikal select the squads which would accompany the ransom train. Taikal himself computed the trail rations and other equipment they would need.

On a bright, chilly morning Taikal drew up his men near the assembled carts and herds. The soldier carrying the captain's standard of two black horsetails that, for the journey, would be Taikal's trotted up beside him. Taikal gave the marching order. Slowly, with many creaks and groans, the laden wagons started up. The herders moved their horses among the herds, shouting and snapping the rope noose at the end of their long rods.

The ransom train traveled three days, fording rivers and filing through hills. When they came to deep woods, Taikal remembered to send scouts ahead to seek, sometimes to make, a road for the wagons. During the first night's camp, one of the lieutenants quietly pointed out to Taikal his poor disposition of sentries and made suggestions for the confinement of the herds. Taikal made no errors in setting up the next camp. At the end of the third day they sighted the Karakhitaians waiting on their horses.

"See how they smirk," Taikal said to his standard-bearer. "They think they have outwitted the Khan."

"They would not succeed with this demand if the Khan did not think well of his men," replied the soldier, a man named Pechen. "Gutchluk does not care how many of his own troops are killed or captured."

Taikal halted the column before a small river. The Karakhitaians quickly rode toward them, splashing through the stream.

Taikal glanced questioningly at Pechen. "Yes, the commander Jiemdad is among them," the standard-bearer said.

Taikal moved his horse up to the Karakhitaian he had met in the yurt of Genghis Khan. "The ransom is here as demanded."

The Karakhitaian grinned broadly and prodded Jiemdad in the back with his sword. "Then take your man and return at once. Gutchluk has no desire for Mongols in his land."

Jiemdad picked up his reins. "You will pay for this insult," he promised angrily. "Do but wait until we meet on the battlefield."

The Karakhitaians took possession of the carts and began driving off the herds. Taikal and Jiemdad trotted toward the waiting Mongols.

"This is a fine place to camp tonight," Taikal said to Jiemdad, pointing out the river and the grassy slopes.

"A good night's march and half of tomorrow will bring us back to our own troops," Jiemdad replied. "I wish to quit this evil land."

"As you desire," Taikal replied. He halted near his three lieutenants and gave orders to move out.

While they waited for the ranks to form, the commander

stared at the cadet. "Who are you?" Jiemdad demanded abruptly.

"The son of Onantu, and cadet officer of Genghis Khan," Taikal replied stiffly.

"What rank does your father hold?"

Taikal smothered his sudden flare of anger. "No rank but that of hero. He died in the Cathayan wars."

Jiemdad jerked his reins, making his horse step away from Taikal's. His lips curled in a sneer. "It is not enough that I must be escorted by only a cadet. But the son of a common soldier!"

The commander kicked up his horse, the long white horsetail that marked his rank swaying as he rode toward the head of the column. Taikal spurred his own mount and caught up in time to hear Jiemdad speak to the standard-bearer.

"What, Pechen!" the commander exclaimed. "You, a captain, carrying a standard for that—that upstart youth!"

Taikal's cheeks flamed with embarrassment. So his standard-bearer was a captain! He remembered how meekly Pechen had followed his orders.

"I volunteered gladly, so I might with my own eyes see you safe," Pechen replied. "See, I have brought your standard."

Taikal noticed now that the familiar standard of two black horsetails had been replaced by the three white horsetails of a commander. Pechen's helmet now bore the black horsetail of captain.

"Well done!" Jiemdad cried. "Are the men ready?"

Anger gave Taikal courage to speak. "I know you are anxious to return to command," he told Jiemdad. "Yet I am in charge of this escort."

"Trouble yourself not with duties beyond your scope," Jiemdad replied coolly. "Take your place at the end of the column. Ride well, son of Onantu, for you will have work to keep up with us."

What, return at the end of the column he had proudly led out from camp? And listen, thereafter, to the other cadets say he had done poorly during a simple errand? Taikal slipped his horse in front of Jiemdad's, barring his way.

"Perhaps you speak truly about my ability," he began. "Yet I can not fail my duty. On the order of Genghis Khan, I am to lead the escort back to camp."

"Out of the way!" Jiemdad made his horse rear up against Taikal's.

The cadet held his place firmly, though hoofs beat the air inches from his face. Jiemdad finally pulled his horse down, and Taikal said boldly, "Should this incident be included in my report to Genghis Khan, or can it be forgotten?"

Blood drained from Jiemdad's face, and he held the reins as if he would snap them.

Taikal called to the lieutenant who had helped him before. "Will you not carry my standard, Kishlik?" He turned to Pechen. "And you, Captain, will be performing a greater service by continuing to bear the commander's standard, but it must be placed behind mine in the column."

Without waiting for anyone to reply, Taikal twitched his mount around. The lieutenant brought his horse up and raised Taikal's standard. The cadet captain gave the march order.

As the horses worked up into a gallop, Kishlik leaned close to Taikal. "It is good that you do not yield easily, lad. Yet I fear that you have made an enemy."

"Here they come!" Taikal sprang up from the evening fire in front of the trail yurt, dropping the boots he had been polishing. He pointed to the distant line of torches which lighted the caravan's path this overcast night. The train began winding down from the hills to the great camp beside the Chensi Nor. The lake itself was glittering with the reflections of thousands of campfires stretched along its shore.

"Let us ride out to meet them," Yarkut said, and he ducked into the trail yurt for saddles and bridles.

Together they ran through the camp, dodging warriors sitting before their fires, slipping between the strolling entertainers and merchants that had put off their journeys to Karakorum in order to join the vast hunt. Beyond the camp grazed the herds of army horses and the sheep and yaks that had recently been brought in. The cadets quickly saddled up and rode out to watch the caravan come down from the hills. Reining in side by side, they saw large wooden wagons rolling behind shaggy, slow-paced yaks whose curving horns reflected the torchlight. Fast-trotting camels drew their carts smartly as their drivers turned them out of line in order to get the best places left in the camp. Horsemen galloped past, shouting and laughing as they tossed their torches up and caught them again.

"Look, tumblers!" Taikal pointed as three men bounced out of a rolling wagon, turning somersaults and back flips before jumping back into the cart.

"Did you not know tumblers were in the caravan you sent from Karakorum?" Yarkut asked.

"Some entertainers left the city with the train, but the rest must have hurried to join the caravan from other parts of the Khan's empire," Taikal answered. While each Mongol tribe would be planning its own fall hunt, this drive conducted by Genghis Khan was to be the greatest in the Mongol empire. Rich profits to be had from twenty-six thousand warriors was a powerful lure to traveling merchants.

A juggler trotted past the two cadets, nimbly tossing wooden balls in a fast circle. On the platform of a cart, lighted with torches fastened to its side, stood two brawny men, flexing their muscles and calling out their prowess at wrestling. Two soldiers resting on their horses nearby at once began laying wagers on the fighters.

After the long train of supply carts and vendors' wagons came the herds of remount horses to be ridden during the drive. A group of horsemen wearing blue cloaks trotted past briskly.

"The Hunt Master and his men," Taikal pointed out. "Tomorrow they begin marking out the drive route."

"And the day after, the hunt begins!"

"Look," Taikal said. "Here come more trained animals."

Barred cages rolled past, their felt curtains rolled up to display the beasts to the warriors who were still riding out to welcome the wagons. While some animal trainers had already joined the camp from western trails north of Kara Khitai, more entertainment was welcome, for the soldiers would be split into three great camps during the long drive.

"See those monkeys that man has brought," Taikal said. "He had just come to Karakorum from Cathay after I sent the caravan out."

"He must have ridden quickly to catch up with the train," Yarkut said.

A wagonload of performing dogs rode by, their barking a thin sound in the confusion of the caravan's arrival. A cage of bears creaked past, the animals growling every time the wagon lurched.

"Are those bears for dancing or fighting?" Taikal asked.

"We have plenty of both kinds already in camp," Yarkut said. "You should have gone with me last night to see Linnam's dancing bears, Taikal. They were very clever indeed."

A messenger galloped up, reining in near them. "Taikal, Chepe Noyon wishes to see you in his yurt," he shouted above the noise of men and animals.

Taikal picked up his reins. "Come with me, Yarkut."

They trotted back to camp and found the field yurt of Chepe Noyon. Unlike the smaller trail yurts, this was large enough to have the cooking fire inside. The evening meal was just ending, and the cadets waited inside the entrance until Chepe's guests had left. The general beckoned the cadets nearer to the fire and signaled his servants to pass around trays of barley cakes and cups of rice wine.

"Welcome, Taikal," the general said. "And you, Yarkut, for you will profit from hearing once again the rules of the hunt. The next eight weeks will be hard ones for you both. As you know, the Khan gives you cadet officers a command during the hunt so he may see how fit you are for leadership. The hunt itself is good training for battle, for you must be prepared for unexpected dangers.

"You must not let a single animal slip through the drive line, whether it be game bird or lynx. No animal may be killed or injured in any way, whether the line is charged by

a snarling wolf or an angry leopard. Never leave behind a
single creature, though foxes go to ground and bears flee to
their dens."

Yarkut nodded. "We must set men with mattocks to dig
them out, bring up shields and blunt lances to turn aside
charges, and use cymbals and tipless arrows to start them up
from the grass and woods."

"And during this time," Chepe reminded them, "it is not
enough to conduct yourselves well with the animals alone.
You cadets will have the responsibility of handling men and
their mounts, of seeing to their food and shelter, and of pre-
venting the rules of the hunt from being broken by others.
And when the drive is finished, you will face the greatest test
of bravery."

"The hunt ring," Taikal said.

Chepe Noyon nodded. "Do you know the order of entry?"
When Taikal shook his head, the general explained. "Each
entry will last a half hour. First Genghis Khan goes in alone,
followed by the generals, one by one. Then all of the commanders enter together, and after them the captains take
their turn. Lieutenants will enter in six groups of five hundred each. Then you cadets will enter together."

"Are we all to enter the hunt ring in one day?" Taikal
asked.

"It will take three days, perhaps more, to slay all the game
in the hunting arena," Chepe replied. "After the officers and
cadets have had their turn, the troops will enter in groups
of five hundred, that is, five companies at a time.

"When your turn comes, Taikal, you will face the maddened fury of beasts which have been driven for two months.
Then you may use your weapons, but do not be overconfi-

dent or careless! I have seen many an experienced warrior
carried, mangled, from the ring."

"What commands will we have during the drive?" Yarkut
asked, for the assignments would not be announced until the
next day.

"I should make you wait until tomorrow," Chepe said
with mock sternness. "Many of our units lack troops because
of casualties. But the cadets will be given fully manned commands. Yarkut, you will remain in Jiemdad's regiment,
riding with a captain named Hirlan. You will be taking
Hirlan's rank during the drive."

Taikal could guess the thoughts behind Yarkut's broad
grin. His friend would command one hundred men, divided
into ten squads, each with its lieutenant.

Chepe Noyon turned to Taikal. "And you will be a captain also, Taikal." He told him to which regiment he had
been assigned. "And you already know that you will ride
with me."

The general then told them of the disposition of troops
during the drive. After that the talk turned to tales of past
hunts. At last, raising his horn of wine, Chepe said, "Before
you lies a test of endurance and courage. Young men, I
drink to your success!"

Later Taikal and Yarkut wandered among the fires burning before the small trail yurts and the larger field yurts of
the officers. Horns were lifted in toasts; men joked and
laughed, and occasionally a boastful shout rang through the
night. Wrestlers, animal trainers, lute-singers, and jugglers
demonstrated their skill to groups around fires, scooping up
the coins tossed to them before running on in answer to
another shouted invitation.

"Jiemdad entertains lavishly," said Taikal, glancing through an open entrance. A large crowd of men was seated on rich rugs around the fire in the commander's yurt. Servants went among the guests with platters of meat and rice cakes and horns of wine. Many of the soldiers, among them Pechen, displayed gifts of arms or jewels that their host had given them.

"Those are men of his command," Yarkut said, as music suddenly struck up within the yurt. Jiemdad's guests jumped up and began stamping their boots to the lutes, fifes, and drums. "He wishes his troops to think well of him in spite of their capture and his own ransoming."

"It is well that I am not under him during the hunt," Taikal said. "He would lose no opportunity to embarrass me because I insisted on keeping command of the ransom escort."

Yarkut nodded. "That is true. But his anger was not due to your father's rank, Taikal. Jiemdad would have acted the same way to anyone sent to ransom him." He pulled his friend's sleeve. "Come, let us watch the shadow play and then go back to our yurt. Tomorrow begins early, for there is much work to be done before the hunt begins the day after."

Drums rattled at dawn two days later, bringing the camp to eager wakefulness. Taikal and Yarkut hurried to strike their trail yurt for the supply wagon to pick up. They were already on their horses with full hunting equipment while the other warriors still shouted wagers on who would start up the first animal of the hunt.

"There is Hirlan, whose place I am taking," Yarkut said. "Good luck, Taikal." He trotted away to meet the captain.

Taikal hurried off to his own company, leaderless since the last Karakhitaian battle had taken the life of its captain.

Taikal would have to manage the company himself, for Chepe Noyon was too busy at the moment to give advice.

Yesterday before dawn the Hunt Master and his men had ridden ahead to mark the route of the drive. The army itself had split into three great divisions, riding off to their positions. The right division, commanded by Chepe Noyon, stayed in the camp by Chensi Nor. Bayan took the left division, and Subotai was in charge of the center. Genghis Khan had moved out with Subotai, but Taikal knew it was the Khan's habit to appear unexpectedly at any part of the line.

Herdsmen snared mounts and sent boys running with them to waiting soldiers. Wicker shields, cymbals, and padded weapons were distributed from the supply wagons. Each man already had the trail rations given to him the night before—a slab of dried meat to place beneath the saddle where it would soften during the ride, a sack of dried milk curds filled with water to be churned into a refreshing drink by the movement of the horse, and bags of cooked rice or barley to hang on the belt.

Taikal had taken part in the hunts of his tribe, but he had never seen anything like the discipline and greatness of this drive. Twenty-six thousand horsemen were to line up in a shallow arc, embracing nearly thirty miles of countryside. They would drive forward for two months, following the white pennants planted by the Hunt Master's men. During that time the right and left divisions would gradually close to form a circle at the point selected near Karakorum. In the last few days, the riders would close up ranks, and horsemen would gradually drop out until a hunt ring of two miles in diameter had been formed.

A lieutenant rode up to Taikal to report his squad ready. The cadet recognized him as Kishlik, the one who had given him advice on the ransom train. Now he made a few quiet suggestions that made Taikal feel less helpless in his new position of responsibility. When the drums rapped out the orders, the cadet already had his one hundred men lined up in his section of the drive. Next to him was the man bearing his captain's standard, and beyond him was a warrior whose saddle drums were ready to transmit Taikal's commands.

Chepe Noyon slipped his horse into line beside Taikal. "You have done well," he said approvingly. "Do not think I was too busy to watch you."

Chepe Noyon waited for the messengers of the ten regimental commanders to report their readiness. Though Taikal sat next to the general, he had sent his company's report to his own commander. When the last regiment was in position, Chepe Noyon sent a fast rider to report to Genghis Khan in the center division.

Taikal waited for the marching order, holding his eager horse in check. He glanced down the line, seeking Yarkut, but not knowing which of the red cadet crests was his. Of the more than one thousand officers in the right division, fifty were temporarily displaced by their sons or assigned cadets.

At last the message from the center came, and the signal was given. Horns blared, and drums snarled. Taikal called the order to his company. The men started up their mounts amid shouting and crashing of cymbals. A great cheering rose from the merchants and entertainers following the camp. Ahead the grass parted in quick zigzags, and nearby a covey of quail exploded. The hunt had begun!

Taikal's excitement was soon submerged in the hard work of minding both his company and the animals which fled ahead. The grass stirred from time to time, marking the flight of hare or fox. Again and again Taikal stifled the warning that rose in his throat as an animal veered from the drive line.

Just before noon the drive left the plain and entered the thickly forested hills. Now they had to go more slowly, rooting out animals which had fled to their burrows. Mattocks flew, and wicker shields were often massed while men shouted and clashed cymbals to turn hares and other small game which tried to slip through the line.

Suddenly a cry rose from Taikal's right. He stood up in his stirrups, peering through the trees. "What is it?" he shouted to the lieutenant nearest him.

"A boar has charged the line!"

Taikal turned his horse out of line and made his way between the trees to where a knot of men and mounts was struggling and pushing while the drive line sagged and threatened to break. Taikal quickly sent a man for shield-bearers. When they came, the men flung themselves out of the saddle and thrust forward against their shields. Two other soldiers prodded the animal with their padded lances. The grunting of the tusked boar changed to an outraged squeal as the warriors, bracing their feet against trees, slowly forced the animal back.

The drummer rattled out the orders, and the line came back into form. At last a triumphant cry told Taikal that the boar had turned and fled into the forest. When the soldiers had remounted, Taikal ordered the drive continued.

"Not badly done," said Chepe when Taikal slipped back into his place. "But you must learn to think more quickly. I was almost ready to give the halt order myself when I heard the drums."

"There are too many things to think of at once," Taikal said. He was glad now he would learn to command during hunts, where mistakes could not result in enemy victories.

Twilight found the drive line still in the forest. Taikal received a message from his commander, then ordered his company to light torches. "The Hunt Master says this night's camp is only half an hour's ride away, Chepe," he said.

"I know, for I received the message not long ago," the general replied.

"Why did you not tell me then?"

"Lad, you ride with me, but you must still receive your information through your superior officers," Chepe replied. "Do you think you will always be conveniently near a general?"

"It was a convenient place to be when we entered the forest," Taikal said. "I had not thought of sending the company's carts around the woods until you suggested it."

Flickering torches spilled wavering blotches of light through the forest. The going was much slower now, for a path between the trees was hard to pick out in the dark.

From time to time a shout for "Mattocks!" told of an animal entrenched in its burrow. The line was held back until the warriors had dug the animal free and chased it ahead through the trees.

At last the woods thinned, and the line dipped into the valley of a narrow, clear river. The carts and herds had already arrived, their route through the winding grassy valley making for faster travel.

Taikal held his company in the line until men brought up extra mounts and picketed them flank to flank. Sentries were posted, and the tired horses used during the day were set out to graze beside the river. Taikal saw to it that his company was supplied with their trail yurts and blankets. Then he selected the men who would butcher the sheep they would eat that night.

The length of the valley was soon lighted with cooking fires. Entertainers roamed among the yurts, and merchants went from warrior to warrior with their goods.

Taikal found Yarkut already turning a sheep haunch over the fire outside their yurt. He flung himself wearily on the ground, glad that the valley grass was cool and damp after a hard, hot day. "It is not the work itself—" he began.

Yarkut nodded. "I know. It is that you are responsible for the men and for the drive too. I am glad this is my second hunt. I hardly enjoyed the first one for worry over my mistakes."

After they had eaten, Taikal and Yarkut went to watch a Cathayan put his trained bears through their tricks. In spite of his great tiredness, Taikal found himself laughing at the huge clumsy animals dancing to the whine of a one-stringed fiddle and turning somersaults around the campfires. Gladly he threw their trainer a few pieces of silver, for the Cathayan had taught them well.

"He is the Lin-nam of whom I told you," Yarkut said as they went back to their yurt. "He told me that when he was a boy in the Sung Empire of southern Cathay a great flood destroyed the family's farm. His father then took them to Kara Khitai, where he learned to manage bears and taught Lin-nam the same trade."

"It is not a bad living to travel thus from place to place," Taikal said. "But what is Lin-nam doing here with the Khan's troops?"

"He said things in Kara Khitai changed greatly when Gutchluk usurped the throne," Yarkut replied. "Gutchluk's administrators demand money freely from any caravan passing through their territory. Even when Lin-nam took his bears among the Karakhitaian troops, he found himself abused and cheated. At the end of this season's fighting he thought it better to leave the country entirely."

"He will find more hospitality among us," Taikal said.

For two weeks the drive continued, steadily advancing, the ends of the line curving inward ever so slightly according to the route planned by the Hunt Master. Each day the line passed more of the white pennants which marked the course. Now and then Taikal had to stop his company while men dug out marmots, foxes, or ground squirrels. Occasionally a startled deer or a defiant wolf charged the line, to be turned back with shield and blunt spears. Twice, black bears had to be prodded out of their caves. And often tipless arrows rained through the air to stir up those low-lying game birds which were not chased ahead by the cries of the men, the beating of drums, and the crashing of cymbals.

The drive went over steep hills, level plains, through rivers and forests. More game was to be seen ahead each day as the fleeing animals increased in numbers.

Taikal was now able to give the right orders without hesitation. But he still became excited over every animal that turned against the hunters, for to allow anything to slip through brought the disgrace of breaking a hunt rule.

One morning Taikal awoke before the drum raps. He tossed restlessly in his blankets, then dressed and went outside to light the breakfast fire. Yarkut soon joined him.

"Today will be a hard one," Taikal said, handing his friend a slice of warmed-over mutton.

Yarkut nodded. "I, too, am worried about those cliffs." He pointed ahead, beyond the line of picketed horses that marked the drive's position. A heavily wooded ridge stretching far to the north rose up before them. On the south the ridge broke sharply into jagged cliffs, their feet buried in a tumbled mass of boulders that fanned out into the valley. "My company begins well past the cliffs," Yarkut said. "But the Hunt Master reports that the ridge and its cliffs turn southward after a good two hours' drive."

"I must take my men right up along the edge this morning," Taikal said. "Some will have to go without horses and explore every cave and crack in the cliffs. Last night I had rope given to them."

When Taikal assembled his men in line, he found Chepe Noyon already at his place. Slipping his mount beside the general's, he found Chepe in ill-humor. "I am not accustomed to wait until cadets choose to join the drive," he said coldly. "You were so busy talking with your troops that you missed the advice I was prepared to give you."

Taikal glanced at the general in swift surprise. His astonishment grew as he noticed an odor, a thick, pungent scent.

"Do not ask!" Chepe commanded as Taikal was about to speak. "Ill-fortune has made me the butt of jokes since that fool of a perfume merchant blundered against my horse, spilling his wares. There was not time to saddle another mount."

"Was it a joke then?" Taikal asked.

"It was clumsiness," Chepe retorted. "The man stopped me as I was riding through the camp, issuing my orders for the day. He tried to press his wares upon me, saying they would make fine gifts for my wife and daughters. In his eagerness he spilled a bottle of scent over me, my saddle, and my horse. I have sent him away from the drive. This wretched scent, however, remains."

"Perhaps we will soon cross a river," Taikal suggested hopefully. As long as Chepe's bad mood lasted, Taikal would have no help in dealing with the problem of the cliffs.

The general chafed impatiently until the last regiment had sent its report. Then he gave the order. Drums rattled; horns sounded, and the drive started.

Taikal's heart was thumping as his company approached the cliffs. Chepe rode on, scowling straight ahead, offering no comment. Taikal sent a message to his commander, stopping the line while part of his company dismounted and began clambering up the debris at the base of the cliffs. He left his usual place beside the general and trotted back and forth near the cliffs, anxious for his men's safety, and fearful lest an animal slip through. He returned when Chepe sent a sharp message.

The general gestured at the thick woods through which part of the line was struggling. "A man can scarcely get through here, let alone a horse."

"What am I to do about it?" Taikal asked, uncertain of Chepe's reply.

"Order them to use their swords to hack a path through the underbrush," the general said shortly.

"But weapons are not to be used during the hunt," Taikal protested.

"They can be used," Chepe replied. "But not on game. Give the order."

Taikal set his company to hacking its way through the thick forest growth, then went back to the cliff. A man fell, injuring his leg. Taikal sent for a physician's cart. Another warrior cut himself badly on sharp rocks but insisted on continuing after his injuries were bound up. Taikal had him mount and take his place in another part of the line. As the cliffs swung southward, Taikal brought his men up on the ridge. Soon the treacherous rocks would be Yarkut's worry.

"The men are going too slowly," Chepe complained as Taikal took his place beside the general.

"After these woods we will cross a river," Taikal said. At Chepe's questioning glance he added, "As the scent is washed away, I think your humor will return."

The general only grunted, but after that he was less sharp with Taikal.

The ground leveled, then pitched downward as they crossed the backbone of the ridge. Often men had to fling themselves out of the saddle to keep their horses from slipping on the steep hill. At last they broke free of the trees. Before them was a gentle slope leading to a river. Suddenly Taikal raised himself in his stirrups.

"Chepe, what is that animal over there?" He pointed to a furred beast which lumbered along the near side of the river. "It is black and white. I have never seen anything like it before."

Chepe followed his pointing finger. "Nor have I. Perhaps it is a new kind of bear."

"Will it charge the line?"

"It seems not to notice us. Wait! It is turning this way!"

The bearlike animal, white with black legs and shoulders, was sniffing the air. The drive line was closer now, and Taikal could see a sudden shudder of muscles beneath the fur as the animal faced the riders.

"Ready spears!" Taikal shouted to his company.

Padded lances swung down, firmly braced in soldiers' arms. Then the strange beast sprang forward. It ran toward the line as fast as an antelope. The small black ears and black circles around the eyes gave the creature a mild look belied by the huge curved claws flashing in the sun as it bounded forward, straight for the cadet captain.

"Shields!" Taikal cried. He turned to the drummer riding close by. "Sound a Slow March." He hardly heard the rap of the drums, fascinated instead by the shaggy beast speeding toward him, its muzzle wrinkled to bare its sharp teeth. Here was the test of the hunt. He must pass it or die. He was glad Chepe Noyon was beside him.

Then while the shields were still massing to meet the charge, the animal swept up in a blur. Taikal's horse reared. The strange beast sprang at Chepe Noyon, slashing his mount with its iron-hard claws.

"Chepe!" Taikal cried.

The wounded horse screamed and reared away. Chepe's padded spear was shaken from his grasp as he fought to stay in the saddle.

Then the black and white beast leaped again, higher this time, the claws aimed for Chepe Noyon's throat.

There was no time to turn the beast with padded spears or to thrust a shield before its victim. No time for Chepe Noyon, rearing on his screaming horse, to leap clear of the driving claws.

Without thinking, Taikal snatched his sword from its scabbard. Seeing only the narrowing gap between the animal's cruel claws and Chepe's throat, Taikal barely felt the impact of sword on bone shudder through his arm.

Hardly realizing what he had done, Taikal found himself staring at the creature near his mount's hoofs. Blood stained the fur where it was white; the muscles gave a last great shudder, and then the beast lay still.

A low moan broke the sudden stillness, and Chepe slipped from his horse. His arm, bare below the short sleeves of his deerskin shirt, was ripped from shoulder to wrist where the claws of the falling animal had slashed him. His face was twisted with pain as he tried to rise from the ground, then fell back, unconscious.

"Help him!" Taikal cried. "Someone help him!" He pulled his scattered wits together and pointed to some of the warriors. "Take him to a physician's cart at once. You others close up the line."

The drive line was tightened up and the steady advance continued while Taikal was left behind with a handful of men. One of these took off his cloak, and with the help of three other men, began carrying the wounded general back to where the carts and herds had rejoined the line after going around the ridge earlier.

"What is to be done with this animal you have slain?" one of the remaining warriors asked Taikal.

An animal killed during the drive!

Taikal's heart drove into his throat as he gazed at the fallen carcass. He heard men coming up from behind. Entertainers, artisans, and other followers of the drive had been attracted by the commotion. Taikal gestured vaguely. "It was going to kill Chepe Noyon," he said.

There was no voice raised in approval or defense.

Taikal said angrily, "He is one of the Khan's greatest generals. What is a hunt rule against the man's life?" Yet he knew the hunt was designed to train men to face death in battle.

Suddenly a chord was struck from the strings of a lute. The notes shimmered in the silence, then a hand stilled them.

Glancing up, Taikal saw a young lute-singer astride his horse. The minstrel was gazing thoughtfully at the carcass of the strange animal, and his hand had seemingly struck the notes without thinking.

"Shall we leave this beast here in the field?" the soldier asked again.

Taikal glanced at the impassive faces of the men around him. "Bury the animal," he said shortly.

A hand tugged at his felt cloak, and he turned to face a trio of scholars. "If it please the young officer," said the man who had pulled his cloak. "Let us be given the carcass, for in all our years of study, none of us has seen or heard of such an animal. We wish to examine it."

"Then take it." Taikal turned to his horse, which had gotten a stone in its foot during its frenzied rearing when the beast had attacked.

"I fought with Onantu in Cathay," murmured a voice nearby. "I did not think his son would be as easily frightened as a girl."

"He is but a lad, and this is his first hunt," another answered more kindly. Taikal recognized the voice of Kishlik, the lieutenant who had often helped him. "Did you not know that once Commander Jiemdad was overly cautious in meeting the enemy? Now the Khan counts him among the first in battle."

Taikal mounted and quickly trotted back to the drive line, leaving the other warriors to catch up by themselves. Kishlik joined him in the line. "You must send a report to Genghis Khan," he reminded Taikal.

"Did you see everything that happened?" the cadet captain asked. At the lieutenant's nod Taikal said, "Then go and relate it to the Khan."

And perhaps, he thought as Kishlik left, perhaps the Khan would make this the one exception. For without Chepe Noyon's inspired leadership, the defeat of the Karakhitaians would be very difficult next year. Surely, if the Khan paid such high ransom for Jiemdad, he would excuse Taikal for saving the life of one of his greatest generals.

Taikal got his company safely across the river and straightened his section of the line as the drive moved across a long grassy plain. As he worked, he waited anxiously for the reply to his report. Meanwhile he found that none of the usual banter of the hunters was directed toward him. Taikal suddenly realized why Chepe seldom minded a jest. Jokes were often a way of expressing friendship, though on occasion they could be thoughtless and cause anger, such as the anger Chepe had shown earlier that morning.

Lieutenant Kishlik returned. "The Khan says you are to report to him after the evening meal."

"Did he seem angry?" Taikal asked quickly.

"I could not tell, for his expression did not change as he heard my tale."

"Take my place for a while, Kishlik," Taikal said. "I wish to see how Chepe Noyon is."

He trotted back to the lumbering cart of the physician who was following this section of the drive. A trail yurt mounted on the heavy wooden platform sheltered both patient and medical man while the physician's servant drove the plodding long-haired yaks. Tossing his reins to the driver, Taikal jumped on the wooden platform and stooped to enter.

The yurt was gloomy, for the smoke hole was closed. A bowl of flaming oil, swaying on three chains from the roof, shed a feeble light. Chepe looked very still. "How is he?" Taikal asked the physician.

The medical man shook his head. "He sleeps. The wound is bad, but he will recover. His arm will be useless for a long time, though he will be able to enter the hunt ring six weeks hence."

"Will he be awake tonight?"

The physician shrugged. "Perhaps. He is strong, this Chepe Noyon. He does not appear to feel the pain. It was the loss of blood which made him fall from his horse."

That afternoon Taikal noticed that some of the lieutenants under him anticipated his orders, as if fearful that the cadet captain would fail to make the right decision. It would be different when Chepe's wound was known to be serious, Taikal thought. No matter what the Khan thought, the silent warriors around him would see that sometimes rules must be broken.

Taikal was very tired when the campsite was reached, the extra horses picketed, guards set, and trail yurts raised. Wearily he gave the last orders for the night and made his way to his own yurt.

"Is it true what the men are saying, Taikal?" Yarkut asked as his friend slumped down next to the fire. "Did you really slay an animal?"

Taikal took the meat and barley cakes his friend handed him. "Yes, it is true." While they ate, he told Yarkut how it had happened. "Think ill of me if you wish, Yarkut. But I could see only the claws reaching for Chepe Noyon!"

His friend nodded gravely. "What does Genghis Khan say of this?"

Taikal scooped up sand and scrubbed his hands clean. "I will find out shortly."

Taikal galloped swiftly to cover the dozen miles separating Genghis Khan's court at the center from his own place in the right division. Even in the night it was easy to find the large yurt of the Khan. The huge white dome caught the color of the many campfires, so that it looked like the flesh of trout Taikal often had caught in his northern rivers.

Giving up his weapons to the Khan's guards, Taikal entered and walked the length of the white horse skin to the brightly lighted throne where sat Genghis Khan. Remembering the time when the Karakhitaian had knelt before the throne, Taikal wondered if now the Khan's scorn and anger would be directed toward him. Reaching the carved lacquered throne, Taikal bowed low.

The great Mongol leader was dressed in his customary felt trousers, simple boots, and plain jacket. Only his rich fur cloak and jeweled belt hinted at the might of his empire, stretching from beyond the Altai Mountains to the Yellow Sea.

At Genghis Khan's side scholars sat on low stools with their writing boards, brushes, and inkpots, while at their feet stood baskets of rolled parchment.

"I have considered the report you sent me this morning," the Khan said sternly, his red beard reflecting the dancing flames of the braziers. "Taikal, you have broken the most important rule of the hunt."

"But Chepe Noyon was in danger of his life!"

Genghis Khan nodded thoughtfully. "Perhaps so—perhaps not. I know well his courage and strength on the battlefield. He has been in hunts for many years, and time after time he has turned a vicious charge without so much as harming a man or an animal."

"His wound is serious, O Khan," Taikal said. "When I slew the animal, it was leaping for Chepe Noyon's throat."

"Had you been prepared, the beast could not have gotten that close," the Khan said.

"I was as prepared as anyone could be, not knowing the animal," Taikal insisted, suddenly aware that he was daring to argue with Genghis Khan. "But even Chepe Noyon was taken by surprise with its furious attack. It was no ordinary beast, O Khan! Surely our ignorance of its nature should not permit the death of your most valiant general."

"It is true my scholars can tell me nothing of this animal," the Khan said. "Yet officers must be able to deal with the most unexpected treachery, whether committed by man or

beast." His voice softened. "You are young, Taikal, and perhaps I gave you too much responsibility."

"Am I to lose my post?" he asked in a low voice.

"One of my commanders has asked if he might have you in his regiment," the Khan said. "He is willing to teach you the elements of proper conduct by letting you lead one of his squads. Tomorrow morning you are to report to Jiemdad."

Riding back to the right division, Taikal tasted bitterness. To lead a squad of ten men was better than nothing, but now Jiemdad had him in his regiment. Taikal remembered Kishlik's words as the escort column had galloped back to camp: "I fear you have made an enemy."

As Taikal guided his horse through the maze of yurts and campfires, he saw a crowd of soldiers struggling to erect Chepe Noyon's large field yurt. So the general was well enough to leave the physician's care!

Taikal found the cart of the medical man. A bellow of anger told him that Chepe was indeed improving. Taikal jumped up on the platform and ducked through the low doorway.

"I will leave as soon as my yurt is set up!" Chepe roared to the physician who tried to quiet him. "Out of my way, purveyor of powders, merchant of misery! Get me my clothes, bone binder!"

Chepe's arm was swathed in bandages and held securely by a sling. He was much changed from the still form of that afternoon.

"I am glad you are much better," Taikal said, coming closer to the general's pallet.

Chepe Noyon's face darkened. "Have you come to laugh over my disgrace?"

"Disgrace?" Taikal repeated in confusion.

"For some time now," the general thundered, "men have been scrambling in here to tell me I was wise indeed to have you nearby to kill that beast, should my pretense at bravery fail. Pretense! I, the greatest Mongol general, first at the hand of my Khan, need not boast of bravery! Listen well to the lute-singers who chant tales of my deeds. Look at the honors the Khan heaps upon me. How dare they question my courage!"

"They can not be saying such things!" Taikal exclaimed in disbelief. "Surely they do not mean them, Chepe. It is only that they jest as they joked about the scent spilled on you this morning."

"Listen to me, lad!" Chepe shifted to a sitting position as the physician fussed around him. "Knowing well my courage and proficiency in battle, why did you think you had to save me from danger?"

"The beast would have killed you," Taikal said. "Those terrible claws—"

"Bah! Claws or arrows, what does it matter to a warrior such as I? Was it that you hoped to snatch glory a little earlier than the other cadets?"

The taunt stung Taikal. "I thought only of your life!"

"Since you are so quick with your decisions," Chepe said coldly, "you can surely finish the drive without my advice."

"You need not endure my company in the line," Taikal retorted. "I am to ride with someone else, under Jiemdad."

As he left he could hear Chepe Noyon bellowing once more for his clothes.

Taikal burned with anger. Now that the mysterious

animal was dead and Chepe was alive, it seemed that no one, not even the general himself, would admit the terrible danger of that furious, unreasonable, attack. Yet Taikal was certain that if the nature of the creature were known, Genghis Khan would have declared it an exception to the hunt rule.

Perhaps the scholars have learned something from their study of the animal, Taikal thought. He turned his horse toward the edge of the camp where the hunt followers had their shelters. He soon found the large scholars' yurt set on a great cart that needed twenty yaks to draw it. The yurt and its wagon was as large as the household dwellings of the Mongol families which moved with their herds according to the seasons. Nearby were camel carts, filled, it was said, with the various instruments of art and science without which the scholars never traveled.

The men of learning could read meaning into the movements of the stars and trace the source of the great quivering which sometimes shook the earth and opened huge cracks in the ground. They could even explain the Gate of Heaven, that mysterious waving band of light which moved down from the north during the long dark winter. Surely they would learn much from the carcass of the slain creature.

Taikal climbed the platform and, entering, stood uncertainly near the doorway of the yurt. Three scholars were busy with strange instruments and rolls of parchment inscribed with mysterious signs. One of the men was Cathayan, another had come from Persia, and the third was an Arab. The other scholars of this group were probably out collecting plants and stones for later study as Taikal often had seen them do.

Since the scholars did not raise their heads, Taikal coughed politely. The three men glanced up from their work, then rose from their embroidered cushions. "Welcome to our poor yurt," the Cathayan said, bowing low.

"It is for me to bow to men of learning," Taikal replied, repeating the gesture. There were no Mongol scholars, and Genghis Khan was grateful for the knowledge these foreigners brought to his empire.

"How may we serve you, young master?" the Arab inquired.

"This morning you took the carcass of the beast I slew in order to study it," Taikal said. "I wish to know what you have learned. Where did this animal come from? What made it charge so madly? Is there a way such a creature could be approached without danger?"

The Persian scholar held up his hand. "One question at a time! As to the origin of the animal, we can not say. Though, of course, it is a real creature and not a spirit."

"I am not so foolish as to think it was a spirit!" Taikal exclaimed.

"We mean no insult, young master," the Persian hastened to add. "This evening a man came to ask if the beast were not a spirit, for he had heard such talk in the camp."

"We had three such visitors," the Arab gently corrected his colleague. "You were engaged, Iskander, in studying the rocks we collected today and so did not notice."

"Our third guest said that a man who limps is trying to persuade others that he is a spirit-talker," added the Cathayan. "He promises, for payment, to protect them from any other such beasts."

The Persian, Iskander, shook his head sadly. "We dedicate our lives to teaching truth, yet such men as this limper can easily find ears into which to pour their falsehoods."

"It is written," said the Arab, "that cheap wine finds a ready palate."

"A rice bowl must be filled before it is discarded," quoted the Cathayan. "If there is no rice, then it will be filled with stones."

"Young master," the Persian added gravely, "carry with you these words of wisdom."

"I—I thank you for this enlightenment," Taikal said, not at all sure what the scholars had meant. "But have you never heard of such an animal in all your travels?"

"In none of our books is there mention of such a beast," the Persian replied. "We have finished our studies of the carcass, and now we are writing a description of the animal. Perhaps in time we may find someone who can tell us the name of this creature."

Taikal's heart sank. "But is it not a fierce animal?"

"Strangely, it does not bear the marks of a vicious animal which would attack as this one did," the Arab replied. "True, the claws are heavy and very sharp, and the teeth are large and strong. Yet this animal would seem to have the habits of a bear."

"Sometimes bears attack people," Taikal suggested hopefully.

"Bears will attack only if they have no escape," the Cathayan explained. "Then indeed they are fierce fighters."

"Yet this beast began charging the drive line from a distance," Taikal pointed out. "We had not even reached its cave or burrow, if such it had. There was no reason for its savage attack."

The Persian shrugged. "We do not know everything,

young master. We can only study the things around us and try to sense their meaning. Many of the mysteries of the world are still hidden from us."

"Perhaps the animal bore wounds which maddened it," Taikal said.

"There were none, beyond the one which killed it."

Possibly the scholars had not paid much attention to the reason for the animal's savage attack. It might be that any wound, inflicted perhaps by a fleeing wolf, was masked by Taikal's killing blow. "May I examine the skin, scholars?"

The Cathayan bowed. "Our humble apologies, but the pelt has been taken from us."

"Taken! Who has it now?"

"A man sent by an officer came and demanded it. He wished to give gold in its place, but we are not merchants and therefore turned it aside."

"Who is this officer?"

The scholars bent their heads together and consulted. They moved in a private world of their own, paying little heed to the doings of the Mongols around them. At last smiles and nods indicated that the name had been recalled.

"The man had been sent by the commander Jiemdad," the Arab stated triumphantly.

"Jiemdad! Why did he want the skin? Does he know of the beast?"

"Alas!" said the Cathayan, parting his hands in a gesture of ignorance. "Some Mongol officers do not choose to explain but only exercise their right to command."

There was nothing else the scholars could tell him. They bowed deeply as Taikal left the yurt.

Taikal wanted very much to know why Jiemdad had taken the skin of the beast. Yet he knew it would be useless to ask any questions of the man he had made into an enemy.

It was getting late, and many of the soldiers had already retired within their yurts. Only a few entertainers strolled about, seeking vainly for a lively group among the few fires that still burned. Seeing them reminded Taikal of the lute-singer who had come up to gaze at the dead beast that morning. He had touched his strings and then stilled them, Taikal recalled. Minstrels traveled widely, and it might be that the lute-singer knew of the strange animal. Tomorrow evening Taikal would seek him out.

He turned his horse into the grazing herd, then returned to the trail yurt. Finding it empty, he went looking for Yarkut.

His friend was among a small crowd watching Lin-nam's bears perform their dances while the Cathayan vigorously stroked his fiddle.

"What did the Khan say?" Yarkut whispered as Taikal joined him.

"I will tell you later," Taikal answered, still heartsick over losing his captaincy. "But things will not go easily for me in the days ahead."

Even the amusing antics of the bears could not cheer Taikal. He watched dully for a while, then told Yarkut he was going back to their yurt.

As Taikal turned to leave, a soldier came forward and pressed a sword into his hand. He pointed to Lin-nam's dancing bears. "There, my brave warrior! Slay those beasts before they kill us!"

Angrily Taikal pushed the man away. Laughter rang in his ears as he hurried off.

With deep satisfaction in his eyes, Jiemdad looked at Taikal standing before him. "I demand strict discipline and obedience among my troops," the commander said. "Make no mistakes, Taikal. I am not accustomed to let the Khan do my punishing for me."

It was clearly a threat. Taikal wondered for a fleeting moment if he should apologize for having insisted on escorting Jiemdad back to camp. Then he stood a little straighter before the commander. He would not let Jiemdad force him into ingratiation. "With whom will I ride while I lead the squad?"

Jiemdad had sent for Taikal at dawn, before the camp was awakened. He had kept him standing before his yurt while he himself finished a leisurely early breakfast. Now he was seated before the fire, eating nuts and fruits, while Taikal stood before him, tired and quite hungry.

"You will ride with no one until you have proved yourself capable of following instructions," Jiemdad said. "The other lieutenants in your company will from time to time oversee your work."

Taikal knew the officers would make a game of it, giving conflicting advice until Taikal had brought Jiemdad's punishment upon him. He resolved to follow his own common sense during the drive, and any discipline from Jiemdad would at least be deserved. But Taikal wished heartily that he had not slain the mysterious animal.

"You should be grateful that I have given you this opportunity," Jiemdad said. Then he waved his hand in dismissal.

"I am indeed thankful," Taikal answered. The next words came without his bidding. "May I ask if you know the creature which wounded Chepe Noyon?"

"What! Know it? Of course not!"

"The scholars say you wished to keep its pelt." From the gathering darkness on Jiemdad's face, Taikal wished he had stilled his tongue in time.

Suddenly the commander laughed. "There is no mystery about that. The skin is a curious one and perhaps valuable." Again he dismissed Taikal, and this time the cadet left the officer's yurt.

The day did indeed prove a hard one for Taikal. The drive was entering the foothills of the Altai range, and it was difficult for Taikal to keep his squad in pace with the others over the uneven terrain. As he had guessed, two or three other lieutenants rode up to him from time to time with conflicting suggestions. Three or four times their advice seemed so sound that Taikal was about to follow it, but a sharp watch on other sections of the line brought him to his senses.

It was easier to keep charge of his own squad, for there were only nine men to watch. Whenever one swung down a padded lance without an order, Taikal made him put it up and commanded someone else to perform that maneuver. Twice this nearly caused disaster, once when a boar and later a lynx charged the line. But Taikal was determined to stay in command of his unit.

When the line reached a river and his men began crossing, Taikal held them on the bank until the line nearly broke before ordering them into the water. By the end of the long, hard day, he had succeeded in making the squad await his orders, though there was much grumbling and surliness. But in this necessary watchfulness and the welter of decisions, Taikal lost all joy in the hunt.

Wearily he flung himself beside the fire outside the trail yurt where Yarkut was turning a roast over the flames. "Six weeks more of this," he groaned.

"The men are laying wagers on how long you keep your squad," Yarkut told him. "But take heart, Taikal. They will soon tire of the sport. Remember, they want to enjoy the hunt too."

"I wish," Taikal said, cutting a slice of the roast with his knife, "that I had never insisted on leading the escort back to camp. And I wish I had let the beast kill Chepe Noyon. I wish I had stayed in Karakorum."

"Perhaps the Khan will let you have your company back if you do well for a few weeks," Yarkut suggested hopefully.

"While we are wishing," Taikal replied, "let us wish that I can learn enough of that strange creature to make the Khan excuse its killing."

"It was something which wandered from its normal range," Yarkut said. "It could have come from anywhere, and you can not travel over the world looking for it."

Taikal was thoughtful as he untied a milk sack. "There is a lute-singer in camp who, I believe, knows of the animal. At least he must know a song about it, for he touched his strings as he gazed at the carcass."

"Shall we look for him after we eat?"

"I know not his name, and there are many lute-singers in

the camp. But I remember his face well." Taikal carefully
described the minstrel's features. Then after the meal he and
Yarkut separated to search for the man.

As Taikal went through the camp, he was surprised to see
that an occasional yurt showed small felt images hanging in
the doorway. A household yurt in Karakorum might boast
such replicas of the ancient idols for decoration or because of
tradition. But an army on the move dispensed with such
homelike touches.

Passing by a trail yurt heavily hung with felt idols, Taikal
caught the words of two soldiers sitting before the fire.

"Basukor says we must return to the ancient ways," one
argued. "The old gods are weary of being forgotten."

"But the old gods are no more," his companion protested.
"The Blue Sky is the only one. The Cathayans, the Buddhists, the Moslems all agree there is only one Supreme Lord
in Heaven, though they do not agree on the best way to
approach Him."

Curious, Taikal slowed his steps and listened.

"But this Supreme Lord will not share His power with
men," the first said. "Basukor says if we perform the ancient
ceremonies we will gain power from the elder gods and ward
off their wrath if they are displeased with us. That ache in
your shoulder is because your brother-in-law killed a lamb
to the old gods and gained power over you. You must ask
Basukor to speak to the spirits on your behalf."

Taikal moved on. So Basukor was the limping spirit-
talker of whom the scholars had spoken! Taikal was at once
amused and annoyed that some men were weak enough to
listen to such nonsense.

While many singers were entertaining groups of warriors, Taikal did not see the one for whom he searched. Now and then he stopped a wandering entertainer or a trainer begging scraps to feed his animals, but they could tell him nothing.

At last someone recognized the description. "I think he is the singer who often talks with Lin-nam," said a passing wrestler.

Taikal thanked the man and set out to find Lin-nam, when he heard someone call his name. Glancing toward a large group of warriors, Taikal saw them beckoning. Hesitantly he joined them.

"Here he is!" the men cried. "Pechen! Pechen!"

They made a way through their group, and Pechen, the captain who had disguised himself as a standard-bearer in Taikal's escort column, came forward with a bundle in his arms.

"You have done well in your post today, Taikal," said Pechen, when the men around the campfire had quieted down to listen. "You did not let the officers confuse you, nor did you let your squad have its own way. Jiemdad is pleased and sends this gift as a sign of your ability."

"My—my thanks to the commander!" Taikal exclaimed. His thoughts had not done Jiemdad justice, for here the commander was giving him grudging respect. Taikal's ill-will fled. Perhaps he would even give Jiemdad the apology the commander had tried to force out of him that very morning.

"Henceforth wear this cloak as a mark of your station." So saying, Pechen loosened the covering and shook out Jiemdad's gift, coming forward to place it on Taikal's shoulders.

Taikal stood rooted with shocked disbelief, while his ears were filled with the raucous laughter of the watching men.

For in Pechen's hands was the black and white skin of the slain beast. With a quick movement Pechen threw the pelt over Taikal's shoulders.

In a rage of anger Taikal whipped off the insulting garment, flinging it into the fire. Out of the corner of his eye he caught a sudden darting movement. Around him the men began pressing closer. Quickly Taikal pushed his way through them and walked rapidly away from the campfire, the taunts ringing in his ears.

Taikal strode through the camp, looking to neither side as the shouts of the men carried the cruel jest from yurt to yurt, always keeping pace with him until he came to the edge of the camp.

Here the supply carts were kept, and here also slept the animal trainers to be near their beasts. Beyond there was only night and silence where the herds moved amid the tall grass. And here Taikal's wrath cooled into helpless misery.

He stared at the distant campfires, clustered thickly and then spreading out on either side. To the north the fires were only a thin sparkling line. Beyond the hills they ended and sentries kept their cheerless watch. Then yet farther north, Taikal knew, would begin again a thin necklace of campfires, until they clustered in the main camp of the center division. For two weeks he had looked at these fires, feeling proud to be part of a great and important hunt.

And now, tonight, he hated them and hated the men who sat in friendship around the flames.

Someone was coming. In the faint starlight Taikal saw a man leading three bears on chains. He stopped beside a wagon and urged the shaggy brutes inside. It was Lin-nam.

Taikal rose from the cool steppe grass and approached the Cathayan bear trainer. "You have many bears, Lin-nam," he said, now noticing a second cage beside the first. Behind the bars felt curtains were tied in place.

"Too many bears," the Cathayan replied. "And I must do the work myself, for my helper ran away two weeks ago. The sheep-witted boy was frightened by their growling."

"I wonder if you know a minstrel I am seeking." Once more Taikal described the lute-singer.

The Cathayan nodded. "He is always asking me to teach him songs from my home." Lin-nam jumped into the cage and let down the felt covers while a bear affectionately butted his legs. "He travels alone and said he was born in the mountains near Kabul."

"Is that a Persian city?"

"I know not whether it is now, for there is always fighting in that district," Lin-nam replied. He came out of the wagon, and Taikal helped him swing up the heavy door. "The singer comes from a strange race of independent mountain men who know no king. They are fierce fighters, living among their cliffs and slaying any man or animal who may threaten their families. This is why Haroun is brave enough to ride into battle with the Mongols."

"Then he was with the army before you joined us," Taikal said. "It is strange I did not notice him before. His name is Haroun?"

"Yes, though it is not his real one. When he began his travels he fancied the name and took it for his own. If you wish to hear new songs, Haroun can sing them, for he has traveled very widely."

"Where might I find him now?"

"He took my place when my bears tired of performing." Lin-nam gave directions, and Taikal bade him good night.

As Taikal made his way through the camp, he found that

Jiemdad's joke had run its course, though a few warriors made loud references to it as he passed.

"Taikal!" Yarkut hurried up to his friend. "I have not yet found the lute-singer."

"Lin-nam told me where to find him," Taikal replied.

"I heard about Jiemdad's joke," Yarkut said, as they walked on together. "Do not let him goad you into some rash deed."

"If Haroun can tell me what I wish, I care not what the men say now," Taikal answered.

The lute-singer had just finished his song and was leaving the large group around three widely spaced fires as two wrestlers took his place. The cadets hurried up to the minstrel.

"Haroun, perhaps you know a song I wish to hear," Taikal said. "Come with us to our yurt."

"Our payment will be poor," added Yarkut. "But we still have a sack of rice wine and some barley cakes for your trouble."

"Refreshment is payment enough," said the lute-singer. "I have finished my night's work."

Together they went to the trail yurt. Haroun seemed surprised to be invited inside, for the autumn had not yet grown cold. Yarkut brought out the sack of rice wine while Taikal found an extra drinking horn and unwrapped the barley cakes. Yarkut lighted the sheep-fat lamp, then let the entrance flap down.

"When you gazed at the body of the creature I slew yesterday," Taikal began, "you touched your strings as if you knew a song about it. Then you were silent. Did you recognize the beast?"

"I have never seen such an animal before," Haroun replied, tightening the strings of his lute. "Yet my song-gathering has taken me over most of the world, and I have heard many things. Now listen closely.

> *"On thickly wooded slopes a strange beast dwells,*
>   *Men know not its name, though many names they say;*
>   *While strong men scoff, the weaker say their spells,*
>   *Is it god or devil, or of mortal clay?*
>   *White the body as fresh bone,*
>   *Black the legs as lava stone,*
>   *Making den in forests lone,*
>   *Shunning all within its zone;*
>   *While other beasts cower when storm snow is hurled,*
>   *It paces the peaks of the Roof of the World."*

Haroun's voice died away on the last note, and the strings echoed him.

"Surely this is the creature which attacked Chepe Noyon!" Taikal exclaimed. "Is there more to the song, Haroun?"

"No, but I have more to tell," replied the singer, loosening the strings of his instrument. "This song I learned from a traveling Buddhist returning from Lhasa. He told me that in this city such a creature is kept in the Potala."

"Is the Potala the Roof of the World?" asked Yarkut.

"Where is Lhasa?" Taikal wanted to know.

"The Roof of the World is what men call the great mountains of Tibet," explained the singer. "It is said the peaks are higher than your Altai. Lhasa is the main city of Tibet. The Potala is a gigantic lamasery just outside the city, where young men train to become Buddhists. The Potala is so famed for learning that many Buddhists from different parts of the world go there to study."

"So this strange animal is kept in a lamasery near the main city of Tibet," Taikal said.

"And Tibet is south of us," added Yarkut. "Just beyond the eastern part of Kara Khitai."

"Is it possible that this animal broke loose and fled north?" asked Taikal.

Haroun shook his head. "There are more creatures than just this one in the Potala. They dwell, as the song says, in the deeply forested slopes of the mountains where men do not go."

"Then how do men know that it is there?" Taikal asked.

"Perhaps some herders saw such a beast," Haroun suggested. "And two or three other men, who might have been seeking lost horses. A glimpse of a strange animal, a tired watcher suddenly startled—of such stuff are legends and songs born."

"Is the animal fierce?" Taikal pressed.

"I know not," Haroun replied, lifting his drinking horn. "Nor do I know how such a creature came to the Potala. But I can tell you how to travel there if you wish to ask the Buddhists themselves."

"But you say you have not been there," Yarkut recalled.

"True enough," replied the lute-singer. "Yet I always remember travel directions from anyone who will tell me. Who knows when the quest for a song will take me to those very places?" Taking his knife, Haroun began sketching a route on the dirt floor of the yurt. "Tibet is the land of no carts, for the country is so rugged that carts can not be used. Listen well!"

They crowded close to Haroun while he described rivers and mountains and lakes they would meet. "Here, at the

Tsaidam, you will join the caravan trail which runs between Lhasa and the Sung Empire. There is great danger at this part of the trail, but I know not what it is, and you must ask the local people about it." Haroun described the rest of the route to Lhasa.

The cadets carefully studied the rough map, and then Taikal rubbed it out with his boot. "We thank you, Haroun, for your song and your information. I hope we can repay you in better fashion than with a few barley cakes."

"It would be well to forget this song," Yarkut added. "Such things are unpopular with the men now."

The minstrel laughed. "You need not worry that I will tell this to others. I have traveled among many nations, some the enemies of others. I could not survive unless I had the wit to obey the wishes of my hosts. As for payment," he added, "I ask only that you describe your journey to me if you should ever travel to the land of no carts."

When the lute-singer had left, Yarkut said, "If you plan to go to Tibet, Taikal, I insist on coming along!"

"And neglect your command as I would have to neglect mine?"

"There is nothing against appointing men to take our places, as long as the Khan consents to our journey," Yarkut said. "Write to the Khan now for an appointment."

"That would waste time," said Taikal, bringing out inkpot, brush, and a piece of parchment. "I will put our request in a letter and send it to the Khan tonight. We should have his answer tomorrow before the drive begins. Then, if he agrees, we could begin our journey right away." He chewed the end of his brush while he arranged the words in his mind and then began writing the request.

The next morning drums had hardly stopped rattling

when a horseman galloped up outside the trail yurt. Quickly Taikal thrust aside his blankets and scrambled outside. The soldier he had sent with the message last night had returned. Taikal took the parchment the man handed down to him.

"What is the answer?" Yarkut asked, joining Taikal outside. "Can we start now?"

With trembling hands Taikal broke the Khan's seal and unrolled the small scroll. Quickly he scanned the brush strokes, then studied them over carefully.

He turned to Yarkut. "The Khan has refused permission."

Taikal's second day in charge of the squad in Jiemdad's regiment was no less hard than his first. The men tried him often, hoping that their commander's jest the night before had crushed Taikal's spirits.

In the middle of the afternoon Taikal noticed that there was less difficulty with his squad. As Yarkut had predicted, the men were beginning to weary of the sport and were starting to settle back and enjoy the hunt itself. They still did not accept Taikal as one of their group, but at least the cadet lieutenant could now concentrate on the problems of the drive.

That evening Taikal relaxed beside the yurt fire after the meal. Yarkut had gone to buy a tooled leather belt for himself, and he returned excitedly.

"Taikal, another beast such as you slew appeared before the left division today!"

Taikal sat up suddenly. "What happened? Was the animal killed?"

"No, it ran off before the drive line," Yarkut said. "But before that it did kill one man."

"So there were two of the creatures," Taikal said. "Perhaps one was the mate of the other."

"And one is still free to attack again," Yarkut reminded him. "Surely this will change the Khan's mind."

"I hope so," Taikal said. "Yet this is not the first time a man has been killed during a hunt. I am going to ride to the left division to see if I can learn what made the animal charge."

He stopped a passing herdboy and had him bring a horse. Saddling quickly, Taikal trotted through the camp. As usual after a hard day on the drive line, the warriors relaxed with their friends, singing old war songs, or listening to tales of heroism chanted by the lute-singers. Some danced to the tune of flutes and drums, locked arm in arm and stamping their sheepskin boots, as they circled one yurt after another, shouting for friends to join them. Here and there a mock battle raged, fought with the blunted weapons of the hunt and giving rise to laughter as a combatant slipped or fell.

Taikal turned his horse from side to side to avoid jugglers or wrestlers running to answer a shouted invitation. Groups of warriors hunched over games of chance, calling for luck as they rolled wooden cubes. The Cathayan shadow play drew a large crowd, as did a pair of fiercely fighting bears.

"Make way! Make way!" a deep voice bellowed from behind.

Taikal pulled his horse to one side and glanced back. Chepe Noyon's black horse paced majestically through the crowd. The general sat proud and straight, his plate armor brightly polished, the black yak tail waving on his helmet. His bandaged left arm was still in a sling. Taikal was about to speak when Chepe Noyon drew abreast, but the general's cold stare made him hold his tongue.

When Chepe had gone his way, Taikal rode past the stalls hastily thrown up by craftsmen accompanying the right division. A gem cutter bent over his tools; a potter crouched near his wheel; an ivory carver rapidly shaped a piece of work for a waiting Mongol. Other makeshift shops displayed silk garments, furs, boots, and leather goods.

Passing through the wagons and carts at the edge of the camp, Taikal kicked his horse into a gallop. Following the curving picket line, he covered the miles to the camp of the center division. Here the carts and herds at the camp's edge forced him to slow down, but once beyond them he regained his speed, galloping on to the left division.

The left division camp looked like his own, except that Taikal did not recognize any of the soldiers. The cadets he saw were not from the big school in Karakorum but were probably the sons of tribal leaders educated by their own fathers.

As Taikal slowly rode through the camp, he heard many fleeting references to the strange animal. One large group around a fire was earnestly discussing the cause of the savage attack. Taikal dismounted and edged closer.

". . . and after that the beast turned and ran into the trees," one soldier concluded. Glancing up and seeing Taikal, he said to him, "They tell me you cadets learn the newest methods of defense. What would you have done, lad?"

The soldiers near him made a place for Taikal to sit down, and one handed him a horn of rice wine. "I know not the tale," Taikal replied to the question. "I come from the right division and have ridden over to hear the whole story."

Eagerly each man repeated his own version, describing first his position on the line when the attack had come. All agreed that near the end of the day's drive a black and white beast had suddenly appeared from among the trees. "We were in the forest back there," a warrior said, pointing into the wooded hills behind them. "The going was hard, for we had to dismount and hack our way through."

"That was good fortune," another added.

"No, no," a third man insisted. "Had we been mounted, no one would have been killed."

The animal had come charging through the dense brush "so furiously it scarcely touched the ground."

"I wonder," said a warrior who had not yet spoken. "Not long before I thought I saw something white in a large tree ahead of us. But I was busy with my mattock and did not notice if it leaped to the ground."

The others scoffed so heartily that the soldier admitted he must have been mistaken.

The strange creature had hurled itself upon a warrior leading his horse through the trees. The soldier had been raked to death by the cruel claws. The beast had had to be forced away from its victim with many lances and the crashing of cymbals.

"I was closest to the scene," said a warrior who had just joined the group around the fire. "It was because this man thrust himself before the creature that he was killed."

"A foolish way to stop a charging beast," Taikal commented. "It should be done with lances and shields."

"It was to save Bayan," the speaker replied. "The general was nearby on his horse. The brute was rushing to attack him and indeed had leaped up and caught his cloak in its claws when the soldier thrust himself between them."

The group exclaimed over this new information. "Then it was the cloak which really saved Bayan," one declared. "Only that morning someone had given it to him as a luck gift."

"I, too, saw the cloak," added another. "It was an expensive garment, brought all the way from Cathay in a scented box."

The talk swung into other channels, for the warriors were by now tired of the old topic.

Soon after, Taikal left them, leading his horse through the camp. From time to time he paused near other fires when he heard the mysterious animal mentioned, but he learned nothing further.

Pausing to let a limping Mongol cross his path, Taikal found himself near the field yurt of the general Bayan. An officer had just left the yurt and was mounting the horse the guard held for him. It was the captain, Pechen. He was talking to the guard, and now he held out a tattered garment. "A poor gift to so easily show wear," he joked. "That is why I was sent to replace it with another."

The guard examined the rips. "It is lucky only the cloak was lost," he said. "But this was such a fine one!"

That must be the cloak that had saved Bayan from the animal's first leap, Taikal thought. It had been indeed a fine garment, bright red with gold embroidery and edged with tiny pearls. Even from where he stood Taikal noticed the odor of spices in which it had been packed for its journey from Cathay.

Thoughtfully Taikal mounted and started for the edge of the camp. Chepe Noyon had worn bright-red leather breastplates when the beast had charged him. He wondered if perhaps the color red for some reason enraged the strange creature.

He had just reached the carts beyond the camp when a voice hailed him. Turning toward it, he made out in the gloom two large wooden cages, their barred sides covered inside by felt curtains. They were hitched one after the other, with four shaggy yaks harnessed to the front wagon. Riding up to the driving platform, Taikal recognized Lin-nam.

"Young master," said the Cathayan, "are you not with the right division? Then tell me how the land lies and where stands the picket line."

Taikal described the route back to the right division, then asked, "But how did you make your way here tonight?"

"An officer of the right division sent me here yesterday to entertain friends of his," Lin-nam explained. "And now he summons me back quickly in the night. Without guidance I feared I might become lost or blunder through the picket line to be arrested by the sentries."

"It will take you all night to return with two heavy carts for your yaks to pull," Taikal said. "Why did you not leave one behind in the right division? Surely you could hire someone to care for them just one day."

"Ah! That extra cart. It is more trouble for me, though I welcome the pay," Lin-nam said. "It is not my cage, nor are they my bears. At the beginning of the drive the owner purchased wagons and bears from some passing caravan and brought them to camp. He put them in my care, though since my assistant ran off they are almost more trouble than the pay is worth."

"You would do better to hire a Mongol lad who can not be frightened by their growling," Taikal suggested.

"I have made a friend or two and so get some help for nothing," Lin-nam replied.

Taikal bade the Cathayan good night and then settled down to the long, hard gallop back to his camp. Several times he thought he heard another horse riding far ahead of him, but it was not unusual for friends in the three divisions of the army to visit one another occasionally.

By the time Taikal reached the right division, many of the campfires had been put out. It was late, and Taikal was anxious for sleep. To save a long walk, he directed his horse toward his trail yurt, thinking to let it find its own way to the herds. Passing one of the few fires, he noticed a Mongol limping toward the men who sat around the flames. It was the same man Taikal had seen near Bayan's yurt in the left division.

The next day was a hard one for Taikal. Though he had forced his squad to obedience, Jiemdad continually sent the unit from place to place in the line so that it always faced the most difficult terrain. The men grumbled openly, apparently blaming their ill-luck on Taikal's presence. "The spirits are against him," he overheard one warrior say to another. "That is why they sent the beast, but he slew it. Now another beast has been sent. It may appear before us!"

"I fear not," replied his companion. "Last night I purchased from Basukor a charm to ward off evil."

The other men joked with these two about their superstitions. Taikal remembered the little felt idols which had appeared last night in increasing numbers. Basukor was taking advantage of the simpler soldiers. Taikal wondered if he were the limping man he had seen the night before, perhaps the same spirit-talker of whom the scholars had spoken.

The next evening, while Taikal and Yarkut sat eating their meal, they saw a large white yurt mounted on a big cart drawn slowly through the camp. The domed shelter was decorated with mysterious signs in several colors. Many idols, some of wood, some of the traditional felt, hung from strings against the sloping walls. A fire was burning inside the yurt, its smoke columning upward through the hole. From time to time clouds of different colored vapors boiled upward. A silk-gowned Uigurian boy stood on the platform behind the driver. Clashing cymbals occasionally, he was bellowing at the top of his lungs. "At moon-high my master will make a strange announcement concerning his power. Come to hear Basukor, the spirit-talker! Let him ward evil from you and increase your riches. Tonight hear his announcement!"

"Let us go, Yarkut," said Taikal. "I am curious about this man." He told Yarkut about the limper he had seen in the camp of the left division. "Perhaps Basukor is the same person."

"I know that Basukor limps, for I have seen him," Yarkut said. "That is the reason he does not ride in the army."

"When did his injury occur?" Taikal asked.

"Many years ago, or so people say. He fell during some tribal skirmish in the east, and his horse's hoofs crushed his knee. He can get along well enough, but he can not ride in battle."

"When did he join the hunt?"

"He was with us all summer," Yarkut said. "He is an animal trainer, and some officers brought him along to train their horses. He stayed with the supply wagons during the battles. When the hunt began, he bought some monkeys and taught them tricks. But now I see he has found a richer profession."

When the moon was at its highest, Yarkut and Taikal joined the rest of the crowd which swelled around the yurt of Basukor. On the driving platform of his mounted yurt scented woods burned in two brass braziers. A gong stood to one side. Taikal and Yarkut pushed close to the yurt's entrance, for the yaks which had drawn the cart had been turned out with the herds. Many of the people in the waiting crowd joked about Basukor and the foolishness of those who would believe in his magic powers. Yet some of the soldiers gazed earnestly at the empty platform.

"It is moon-high," complained one such warrior nearby. "Yet Basukor appears not."

"Perhaps the spirits have not yet told him what announcement to make," replied his companion with a grin.

"Jest not," warned the first. "Someone insulted Basukor not long ago, and the next day the man was injured by a stone which mysteriously flew through the air."

"I did not know Basukor was accomplished in the art of slinging," returned his friend.

When the crowd's exuberance had finally run its course, the yurt's entrance flap was abruptly thrust aside. Basukor stood revealed in a splendid gown of silver, his head covered by a cap from which stretched two gilded yak horns. The former animal trainer flung his hands outward, and instantly the bowls of fire burst forth with colored smoke. Those nearest the platform fell back in surprise.

"Basukor has chosen his moment well," Taikal observed to his friend. "The crowd has finished with its jokes."

The smoke dispersed rapidly to reveal the Uigurian boy near the gong. The lad struck a somber note, and his master advanced to the edge of the platform with an awkward gait.

"That is indeed the limping man I saw," Taikal whispered. "Not content with the right division, he must also spread his tales in the left."

"Friends," began the magician. "Know that when I was born, an old woman came to the yurt of my mother. Laying her hands upon me, she transferred to me her gift of speaking with the spirits. I kept my ability secret for many years, but now the spirits tell me I must use it to help others."

"He means," whispered Yarkut with a grin, "that only now has he found such nonsense an easy way to earn money."

Basukor went on to describe to his listeners a vast assortment of spirits and gods, each supposedly possessed of a particular power. Some of these Taikal vaguely recognized as old legends he had heard in his childhood. A few others had obviously been born of wild tales brought by caravans from distant lands. The rest seemed to be pure invention.

But he, Basukor, knew all the spirits well. He understood the ways of using or curbing their powers. "Yet I see doubters among you," he proclaimed. "And so I will demonstrate my powers. I will cause a great whirlwind to come and gather the sands of the desert and fling them upon you to clog your throats, stuff your eyes, and stop up your ears. And when the sand scours your skin and you choke on grit, remember that it was I, Basukor, who caused it to happen."

Again the magician flung apart his arms, and once more the colored vapors boiled up from the braziers, one cloud green and the other red. When the smoke cleared, Basukor was gone. The Uigurian boy struck the gong and announced that his master was available for divination consultation and the dispensation of charms to ward off evil spirits.

The crowd began to drift away, though several people pressed forward to do business with Basukor. Among those who were leaving, Taikal saw expressions of outright scorn, but many faces showed a struggle between believing and not believing.

"Surely the men must remember when Basukor was only an animal trainer," Taikal said, as they walked toward a wrestling match.

"Not many pay attention to those who manage the herds and wagons," Yarkut answered. "And of those who do, some will think Basukor really did keep his power to himself until the 'spirits' told him otherwise. Let them throw away their hard-earned pay. It is a harmless amusement."

The next day dawned hot and sultry, unusual at this time of year. The men were on edge, and during the drive the animals showed a restlessness and bad temper that had not been encountered before. Taikal's section of the line was driving up a long valley, and even timid animals turned to face the hunters, trying to charge between the legs of horses. Once a boar came running out of the forest on the hills, charging for Taikal's squad.

The men were slow to act. Taikal moved his horse forward, bracing his padded lance firmly. He felt the shock as the boar flung itself against it. Taikal's horse faltered from the impact, scrambling to dig its hoofs in the ground to keep its balance. "Shields!" Taikal shouted.

The boar snorted angrily, bolting away a short distance, then returning with a powerful lunge. Its wicked eyes gleamed as it poised its dangerous tusks. The shield-bearers had advanced but were not quite ready for the charge.

Taikal thrust his lance between the dismounted men and caught the boar low on its shoulder. The blow flung the animal to its side, and the shields massed to form a solid barrier. The animal attacked again, thudding against the shields. For a moment Taikal thought it would break through, but the line held, and at last the boar turned and ran off, squealing angrily.

"You did not give the order soon enough," complained one of the soldiers as he remounted.

"You would act more quickly if your wits were about you," Taikal retorted. The stifling air stretched nerves taut. Perhaps there would be a storm.

There had been storms before, blasting winds and driving rain that had halted the line while men crouched beneath their cloaks. Then, when the storm had passed, laughing hunters had ridden on, sodden garments drying in the sun.

But today not a breath of air stirred. Men's tempers snapped easily in the unnatural stillness.

Suddenly Taikal raised himself in his stirrups. Far ahead a low yellow cloud was boiling over the hills surrounding the valley. "Sandstorm!" he cried in warning.

The waiting was over.

Officers shouted their orders. Drums rolled, and the line halted. Messengers spurred their horses, passing the word up and down. The supply wagons, taking the easy route through the valley, drove up, and their drivers quickly began passing out cloaks, sections of trail-yurt cover, blankets—anything which would cover the heads of men and horses.

Glancing back, Taikal could see the artisans and entertainers who followed the hunt drawing their carts and wagons together, unhitching the draft animals. Herders hurried yaks, camels, sheep, and extra horses behind the protecting barrier. Flaps were secured over yurt entrances, and men struggled with draw ropes to close the smoke holes.

Taikal went from man to man in his squad, seeing that the mounts lay on the ground, backs toward the coming storm and heads bundled in cloths. Men huddled next to their horses, wrapped in cloaks or blankets. He shouted a warning to one lagging soldier.

Now the yellow cloud filled the sky. Taikal tasted grit as a haze of sand showered over the drive line. He had just dismounted when the wind came, flinging him to the ground in a sprawl. His horse reared and would have bolted, but Taikal struggled up and grabbed the reins.

Fighting against wind and sand, he forced his mount to lie down. Wrapping his cloak around his horse's head, he pressed himself beside the animal.

The wind howled, driving sand into his nose and ears in spite of his horse's sheltering bulk. Taikal buried his face in his arms, clutching the grass to keep from being driven bodily by the wind. His ears seemed to lose their hearing as the storm shrieked around him. There was no telling how long it would last.

The world was filled with stinging sand and howling wind. Taikal lost all sense of time. Suddenly he felt someone flinging to the ground beside him. It was Yarkut.

His friend put his mouth close to Taikal's ear. "Come with me. There will be no time later."

Taikal pulled his friend's ear close. "What is it?"

"I know not," Yarkut shouted in reply. "But there is trickery somewhere." Impatiently he pulled Taikal's sleeve, pointing far down the drive line to his company's section.

Taikal worked his jacket loose from behind his saddle. Wrapping it around his head, he bent into the wind and followed his cloaked friend. It was slow progress, fighting against the tearing wind and blinding sand. Twice he lost his balance and had to drag himself back on his feet. Several times he lost sight of Yarkut when a heavy cloud of dust surged between the two. Only dimly could he make out the huddled figures of warriors and horses as Yarkut led him down the drive line.

Then the ground sloped beneath their feet. At the bottom they splashed through a small stream, yellow with blown sand. There was a cliff on the other side. Yarkut pulled Taikal through an opening.

The press of wind dropped suddenly and its whine was

muffled. Taikal shook the sand out of his jacket. He saw they were in a shallow cave. The entry crack let light in, though it was dimmed by the veil of sand which drove past. A cold stream trickled across the floor of the cave to join the one outside. Taikal stooped and rinsed the grit from his mouth. "You are lucky the rest of the army did not crowd in here," he told Yarkut.

"The drive line is some distance ahead of us," Yarkut said. "I myself went into this cave to see if there were animals hiding here. There were none, and my company passed beyond it. After I got my troops ready for the sandstorm, I remembered what a fine shelter the cave would make, so I sent my horse running back to the herds while I came here. It was then that I noticed these marks."

He pointed to the floor of the small cave and to sections of the walls where black stains marked the rock. "One or two of these spots have hair dried into them."

Taikal examined the stains closely, chipping the crusty black with his fingernail. "This is not mud. It is like lacquer."

"But see how easily it washes off," Yarkut said. "My foot slipped into this stream and splashed water on some of the marks."

Taikal cupped his hands in the cold stream and wet one of the black spots. Stirring it around with his fingers, he found that the black washed away rapidly. "Look, Yarkut. These hairs are really white. Someone has been here and has done something, but what—and why?"

"And remember that the drive line did not pass this point until a short time before the sandstorm," Yarkut pointed out. "And just before that I found the cave empty."

"The spots are dry," Taikal said. "This business was done

some time ago. The only thing I can think of that has white hair is that strange beast."

Yarkut nodded excitedly. "Do you realize what this means, Taikal? Someone is responsible for the two mysterious beasts which attacked Chepe Noyon and Bayan."

The wind whipped up, and sand showered into the cave.

"Someone has used a cheap black dye on a white animal," Yarkut said. "Perhaps the beast was really a white bear from the far north, partly colored to frighten men into inaction while it charged."

Taikal shook his head. "This kind of dye would come off so easily that anyone working with the skin of the beast I slew would show black hands. The scholars did not mention such a thing to me. And when Jiemdad sent me the pelt as a 'cloak,' Pechen's hands were not blackened. Nor were mine when I grasped it to throw it away, though I know my hands were moist with anger. Besides, Yarkut, it would be impossible to take a white animal through the drive line. The sentries would see it easily even if there were no moon."

Suddenly they stared at each other, both struck by the same thought. "It was the white part of the animal that was dyed black!" Taikal exclaimed. "Then the animal could be taken through the drive line with no fear of being seen."

"It must have been done by someone with the drive," Yarkut added. "He would have to know the placement of sentries."

"And he is probably familiar enough with horses to keep them quiet as he went through the picket line," Taikal said. Then abruptly he shook his head. "It would not work, Yarkut. Whoever is doing this would have to have kept the animals with him for two weeks during the drive before releasing the one which attacked Chepe Noyon. It would be impossible to hide such ferocious creatures from the rest of the camp. And besides, why would anyone do such a thing? And where did he get the strange beasts?"

Yarkut shrugged. "I know not. But let us find who has sold such dye as this and to whom. Then we can set about answering the other questions."

"But first," said Taikal, "I want to bring Chepe Noyon to this cave tonight."

When camp was made that evening, everyone seemed to be talking about how Basukor had brought about the sand-storm. Many of those who had struggled against believing in the spirit-talker now accepted his power as fact, though most of the soldiers were not yet convinced. To press his ad-vantage, the former animal trainer promised to make another public announcement that night.

The men were curious enough to hurry through their evening meal, and while Taikal and Yarkut still sat by their fire, warriors began drifting toward the cart-mounted yurt of the magician.

"But we would have ridden into a sandstorm even without Basukor's help," protested one soldier, as he and a friend passed the cadets' trail yurt. "Great windstorms bringing sand from the Gobi are not rare."

"Do not close your mind to Basukor," his companion in-sisted. "Listen to what he will say tonight."

As the warriors passed out of earshot, Yarkut said, "Did you notice that Basukor did not say when he would 'cause' the sandstorm? At this time of the year we were likely to encounter at least one before the hunt ended."

Taikal cut another slice from the roast. "True enough. Basukor was lucky the storm came the very next day after his announcement."

"The storm was lucky for us too," Yarkut said. "We would not have found those mysterious marks in the cave otherwise. How will you manage to see Chepe Noyon? He has not spoken to you for five days."

"He usually rides alone to the Cathayan shadow play, and we can meet him on the way."

When the meal was over, Yarkut went to fetch two horses from the herds while Taikal scoured their eating utensils with clean sand. The sand had almost completely covered the valley grass. The herd animals would have to work for their graze.

After saddling up, the two cadets rode through the camp, watching for Chepe Noyon. Taikal pointed to a large crowd. "Is that the shadow play?"

Yarkut stood up in his stirrups. "No, it is Basukor. See the colored smoke? Let us find what he has to say this time."

They trotted to the edge of the milling crowd. Basukor was cloaked in a gown of silver decorated with spangles of many colors. His cap of yak horns had been replaced by a wolf's head, painted blue. It was a well-chosen symbol, for the Blue Wolf was the legendary ancestor of the Mongols. His face was framed by the teeth of upper and lower jaws, and the magician seemed to be really speaking for the old spirits.

"But because the old ways have been long forgotten," Basukor was saying, "many among you are not yet convinced."

"Let sleeping spirits lie," grumbled a warrior near the cadets. "Life is hard enough without adding to it fear of my enemies' spells."

"Basukor will give you amulets against them," replied the man's companion earnestly.

Basukor was still speaking. "Five days ago a strange animal appeared among you. It was black and white and charged with the murderous fury of the ancient spirits. But in fact it was no earthly beast. It was itself the principal god of all the old spirits who chose this means to remind you to go back to the old ways."

Protests rang from the crowd. "It was slain!" "A common sword killed it!" "It shed the blood of an animal!"

Basukor held up his hand for silence. "It permitted itself to be slain, so you might study it well and observe its strangeness. Who among you can say he has seen such a creature before?"

Taikal's heart thumped. If Haroun would only keep the secret! Hastily he scanned the listeners, but he could not find the lute-singer among them. He did see Jiemdad, and the commander's face was set in a scowl. A murmuring rose from the crowd. From their gestures Taikal could see that many were violently disagreeing, yet the sober nods of others showed that the charlatan had won over more believers.

"What of the second animal?" a man shouted.

"It was the same!" Basukor proclaimed triumphantly. "The spirit yet lived and fashioned for itself another body like the first. I have power over this spirit. And because many of you still do not believe me, I will perform another marvel. When the stars arrange themselves in a suitable pattern, when the sun and moon are as brother and sister in the sky, then I shall summon the black and white beast before your very eyes. And then, if you do not return to the ancient ways and honor the forgotten gods of old, I will send the beast forth to rage among you."

Taikal murmured to his friend, "I have heard enough."

They began easing their horses through the crowd, for more listeners had joined after the cadets had come. "Look!" Yarkut commanded with a gesture.

A white horse stood apart from the crowd, the rider almost indistinguishable in the shadows beyond the fires near Basukor's yurt. It was Genghis Khan.

Even as they watched, he twitched the reins and disappeared into the shadows.

It was the Khan's habit to appear unannounced at various places of the drive line. But this was the first time Taikal had seen him in their camp. "He probably heard of Basukor's sandstorm," he said, "and rode over to see what manner of man the magician is."

"At least now he knows the animal is a spirit and it caused you to kill it." Yarkut laughed as they walked their horses toward the shadow play.

"I fear Basukor's nonsense will only make him angrier than ever at the mention of the strange beast," Taikal said. "Yarkut, there goes Chepe Noyon."

Bellowing his familiar "Make way!" Chepe came pacing on a white-nosed sorrel mare, threading a path through the warriors and entertainers thronging among the yurts. Though his arm was still in a sling, both hands held the reins.

Together the cadets trotted up from behind, slipping their horses one on either side of the general, "so that," as Taikal had whispered, "Chepe must listen with both ears."

The general said, keeping his eyes straight ahead, "I do not remember inviting you to the shadow play."

"This is a matter of great importance," Taikal began. "Yarkut found a cave that makes us think someone directed the attacks of that strange animal I slew."

"We wish you to see it," Yarkut added. "There are marks

of cheap dye, and we think someone disguised the beast and slipped it through the picket line."

Chepe grunted, but whether it was from surprise or scorn, Taikal could not tell. "I know this does not excuse me for killing the animal," Taikal said. "But if someone is playing a trick, you should know of it."

"A trained animal is not subject to the hunt rules," Chepe said. "But do not use this cave as an excuse to make me listen to your apologies. I will not plead with the Khan for you."

"It was not a trained animal, but it must have been in captivity," Taikal said. "Will you come?"

Chepe consented, and they turned in the direction of the cave. Clearing the camp, they worked their horses into a canter.

"It is not far," Yarkut shouted. "We have only to follow the stream in the valley."

A gallop of ten miles over the sand-strewn valley brought them to the place. In the moonlight Taikal gathered sticks for a torch while Yarkut held their horses.

"The line was far back when the first beast appeared five days ago," Chepe objected. "Surely we would have passed this cave sooner, if indeed it was used for the purpose you claim."

"That puzzled us too," Yarkut admitted. "Then we remembered that our part of the drive is traveling in a curve to bring the ends of the line closer together day by day."

"If someone did take the beast through the line," Taikal added, struggling with his fire-striker, "he would probably travel straight ahead a good distance to find a place to wash the dye from the animal. But it would take even longer for our group on the drive to reach the same place, for we travel in an arc. And the drive moves slowly."

The makeshift torch flared and crackled. Taikal led the
way as they crowded into the small cave. "Now you will see
that someone has been using this as a hiding place."

He held the flickering, smoking torch high and waited
for Chepe's startled exclamation.

But it was Yarkut who uttered a cry of surprise. "Taikal!
Someone has been here tonight!"

"Where," Chepe asked coolly, "are these marks you
wished me to see?"

Taikal looked closely at the walls and on the floor of the
cave. "They are gone! See, there are wet spots where the
dye has been scrubbed away."

"It was strange marks I came to see, not water," the general said, his annoyance increasing.

"But, Chepe," Taikal insisted, "do you not see that this
proves that someone is doing something in secret?"

In a rush, lest Chepe close his ears to them, Yarkut explained his discovery of the cave and carefully described the
marks and the white hair which had dried with them.

"We have but to discover who buys cheap black dye,"
Taikal pointed out. "Then we can set a trap for whoever is
responsible for the attacks."

"You lads have much imagination," the general replied
sternly. "If indeed there were black marks here, they could
have come and gone a thousand different ways, with or without the hand of man. Hereafter do not trouble me with such
wild ideas." He strode from the cave, and even as Taikal
extinguished the torch in the clear stream within, they heard
Chepe Noyon galloping off.

More slowly they returned to the camp. "Perhaps Chepe
is right," Yarkut suggested. "We were too anxious."

"The mysterious animals attacked Chepe Noyon and

Bayan," Taikal said, thinking out loud. "It is strange that both men are generals."

"A coincidence," Yarkut replied. "Like Basukor's sand-storm."

"Even if Chepe is right," Taikal said, "and the strange animal had no contact with a keeper, I would still like to know what made it attack in such a savage fashion. One yet lives beyond the drive line. There may be more. How can we be prepared against it if we know nothing of its habits?"

"The Khan has refused us permission to go to Tibet to learn of this creature," Yarkut reminded him.

"Perhaps he thought I only meant to leave the drive line," Taikal suggested. "I would like to ask him again, this time in person so he may see in my eyes the true reason."

At their trail yurt Taikal brought out his writing materials. Using the most respectful terms he knew, he asked for a private audience.

"Did you mention the cave?" Yarkut asked after Taikal had sent the letter off with a messenger.

Taikal shook his head. "He might say the same things Chepe Noyon told us. While we wait for the Khan's reply, let us search for the dye seller."

"There are only five furriers with the right division," Yarkut said. "Most of them are in the center, vying for the Khan's favor with their gifts to him." He counted on his fingers. "There is a Kharesmian, two Cathayans, a Moslem from Damascus, and a Muscovite. I will speak to the first three, for the farther west people come from, the stranger they seem."

"If you find the dye, purchase some of it," Taikal said. "I have an old pair of gray fur boots, and they will look better if I dye them."

Taikal went first to the Moslem. The furrier's only black dye, however, was very expensive. "The color will never come off, young master," the man from Damascus assured him. "I sell only the best."

Taikal politely declined, then went in search of the Muscovite. He found him stitching a cloak in his makeshift shop, which was three or four blankets stretched on a frame of poles.

"How can I help you, young master?" the Muscovite asked as he glanced up. He was probably a new traveler in high Asia, for he spoke in Arabic, the language of the caravan trails, instead of the Mongol or Cathayan common to traders in the eastern steppes.

"I have a pair of old fur boots." Taikal spoke slowly, in the stilted phrases he had learned at school. "They are patched and faded, so I thought to purchase a dye to cover the worn spots."

The Muscovite nodded and dragged forth a chest filled with clay pots. "Here are the dyes I carry with me, young master. This red-brown is a fine shade—"

"I see the color I want." Taikal pointed to a glazed pot filled with the same shade of black he had seen in the cave.

"An excellent choice, young master," the Muscovite approved. "I have several grades of this color, for it is in great demand. Here." He lifted a tray from the chest and selected a pot from the bottom. "This will last a long time and endure through all climates." Apologetically he quoted several pieces of silver.

Taikal laughed. "That is more than my boots are worth. Show me something cheaper."

The Muscovite brought out other dyes, describing their qualities in detail. When he had finished, Taikal pointed to one of the pots that had not been touched. "What is this?"

"Bah! That is the cheapest of dyes, not fit for a young Mongol officer. It is used only by some who would cheat their companions, for the dye runs in the rain. I am sorry I ever troubled to bring it with me."

"If you can not sell it, why not cast it away?" Taikal asked with studied casualness.

"Strangely, I have sold much of it," the Muscovite replied.

"Then tell me who bought it, furrier," Taikal urged. "I surely do not wish to be cheated should I buy a cloak from someone in the camp."

The Muscovite frowned in thought. "Well, at the beginning of the hunt there were two or three. . . ." He moved his lips in an effort to conjure up the names.

"That matters not," Taikal said. "They have surely sold their cheap articles by now. But has no one bought some recently, within the last five or six days?"

"Ah, that I can tell you," said the furrier. "There were four such purchasers. Not long ago I sold some of this cheap dye to the man who calls himself the spirit-talker. Basukor is his name."

Basukor! Why had Taikal not seen this before? It was the first appearance of the strange beast which had given the animal trainer the opportunity to talk of charms and magic. So it was he who arranged the savage attacks!

The Muscovite was still speaking. ". . . and a small quantity to a bear trainer, the Cathayan called Lin-nam. You have but to avoid these four men and you will not be cheated."

Taikal thanked him, then bought a quantity of fairly expensive dye in his jubilance over finding the guilty man. In high spirits he went to look for Yarkut.

"I have had no luck at all," his friend confessed. "The

Cathayans do not carry that shade of black, and the Kharesmian does not sell any of his dyes at all."

Taikal told Yarkut what he had learned. His friend nodded thoughtfully. "That is the answer to why this is being done. For money and power. Basukor was crippled in his youth, when men are just beginning to earn fame and honor."

"And he is, or was, an animal trainer most of his life," Taikal pointed out. "But still, where did he find such a beast as that which attacked the drive line?"

"He has traveled," Yarkut said. "But only to Samarkand and to the Kin Empire of northern Cathay. Yet perhaps he knows where such beasts are bred in captivity."

"We can learn of this in Lhasa," Taikal said, excitement rising in him. "Let us return to our yurt and see if the Khan will allow me to visit him."

They found a soldier waiting for them in front of their yurt. Handing Taikal a scroll, he mounted and rode off.

Taikal broke the seal and unrolled the parchment. He turned to Yarkut with a grin. "The Khan has granted me a private audience. I will have to go at once."

As he galloped to the center division, Taikal wondered how to phrase his request. His best reason for wanting to learn more of the mysterious animal lay in the clue he and Yarkut had found. But since many came before the Khan with complaints and suspicions, it was the Khan's custom not to listen to charges unless the man was named and his guilt proven.

Genghis Khan was alone except for the ever-present scholars. Taikal bowed before him. "I have come, O Khan, to ask once again if I may undertake a journey in order to learn of the mysterious beasts which have twice attacked the drive line."

"Is your disgrace still so hard to bear, Taikal?" the Khan asked, the flickering light of the braziers dancing in the tangle of his long red hair and beard.

"That is not my reason for asking," Taikal replied. "Already a man has been slain by one of these animals, as another one very nearly was. It is my belief that something in the nature of the creature drives it into sudden rage—perhaps a color or some sound. If we knew this, we could be better prepared to deal with the animal." Taikal paused, then plunged ahead recklessly. "Perhaps there is someone who understands this animal and so has a means of directing its attacks. This could be prevented if the secret were known. I—I do not mean to accuse anyone."

The Khan nodded thoughtfully. "The world is large, Taikal. Where would you go?"

Taikal knew that if he mentioned Haroun, the Khan might question the lute-singer. He did not know if Haroun's custom of keeping out of trouble would make him deny the song he had sung. "I have heard of the scholars near Lhasa," he replied. "Nothing is too great or too humble for them to study. Surely they must have knowledge of this odd creature."

The lines between the Khan's eyes deepened as he thought over Taikal's request. "Have you spoken of this to others?"

"Only to my friend Yarkut. He desires to accompany me on the journey to Tibet."

"The nature of the beast matters not," said the Khan. "Warriors must be prepared to meet any emergency upon the battlefield. Yet there is one who seeks to take advantage of this strange animal—Basukor, who calls himself a spirit-talker."

Taikal remembered the Khan's appearance at the edge of

the crowd that night. Had Basukor's words so angered him that he was annoyed by the very mention of the black and white beast? "He is a man of false words," Taikal said.

"Do you understand the difference between religion and superstition, Taikal?" the Khan asked. "How do you know that Basukor is an unworthy man?"

Taikal thought hard. Basukor's foolishness seemed so obvious that he had never studied the reasons behind his opinion of the charlatan. "He was an animal trainer until the first beast appeared and gave him the opportunity to speak fear into those who listened to him."

"Yet there are many holy men in Karakorum and other parts of my empire," reminded the Khan, "who come from humble lives. One very wise Nestorian was a herder. A renowned Buddhist once harvested rice. A Moslem was born a slave."

"That is different," Taikal protested. "These holy men studied under the scholars of their religion. And they do not sell charms and spells."

The Khan nodded. "They do not trade upon fear, but only warn that a man may earn his own punishment from the Supreme Lord, Whom we Mongols call the Blue Sky. But is there not another difference?"

"They are kind," said Taikal. "Often I have seen them give food and clothing to others who had nothing. All they ask in return is that this favor someday be passed on to another who is less fortunate." Taikal's mind cleared suddenly. "I know the difference! Nestorians, Buddhists, Moslems, and even the occasional Franks from the Far West all teach us to lead good lives."

Genghis Khan nodded. "They teach us a code of conduct. But some find it hard to live in truth and honor, and it is these weaker ones who listen to Basukor's falsehoods. Truly he offers no religion but is interested only in money and power. If Basukor succeeds in bringing back superstition, he will also destroy man's trust in man. He will ruin the empire and destroy the code of laws it took us so long to formulate."

"But surely not everyone will believe in him!"

"True, yet there are many ambitious men who would pretend belief in order to become leaders of those flocking around this 'spirit-talker.' Have you not heard of Taib-tengeri? He was a man who several years ago pretended to be a magician, as does Basukor. He incited malice, envy, and ambition until he turned many good men against me."

Taikal had heard whispers of that conspiracy which had come very near to taking Genghis Khan's life. Though Taib-tengeri had been slain and his body spirited away, the Khan had lost forever some allies, whom he later had to defeat on the battlefield.

The Khan continued. "It is even likely that Basukor's superstitions could so divide the troops that we would lose next summer's war with the Karakhitaians. We have struggled long and hard to establish a united and orderly empire, where fear and poverty are little known, and where wisdom and truth are welcome. Basukor could change all this. For this reason I seek to discredit his 'magic.' Therefore, go. Learn what you can of this mysterious animal, so that it can be proved it is not a spirit as Basukor claims."

Taikal grinned broadly as he stood up. "Yarkut and I will leave this very night."

"Tell no one where you go, nor the purpose of your going," the Khan warned. "If Basukor learns of your errand, he might find a way to hinder your journey. Send me a report upon your return. The journey should take no longer than a month."

"Perhaps the scholars in Lhasa will direct me to another place," Taikal suggested.

"You are to return as quickly as possible," the Khan replied. "If you can not learn of the creature in Lhasa, further search is useless. Then I shall have to deal with Basukor in my own way."

When Taikal reached his own camp, he turned his horse loose among the herds. Then, carrying bridle and saddle, he walked casually to his yurt, as if he had only ridden out to visit some friend.

Haroun was sitting by the fire, talking to Yarkut. He greeted Taikal with a nod and a chord from his lute. "The evening is dull," he said. "Everyone talks of nothing but Basukor's prediction, and no one will listen to songs tonight."

"You might have a new song to sing when we return," Taikal said.

The singer leaned forward. "Then you are going to Tibet after all!" he exclaimed in a low voice.

Taikal instantly realized what he had done. Yet it was Haroun who had told them of the beast kept in the Potala, and the singer would easily guess their destination when it became known that he and Yarkut had left. "Yes, we are going. But, Haroun, it must be kept a secret, or it will go ill with all of us."

Haroun drew up one leg, his hand caressing the black fur boot. "Basukor asked tonight if anyone knew of the mysterious animal," he reminded them. "Had I chosen, I could have come forward. But I never become involved with the plans of my hosts and so said nothing."

"Grant us a favor, Haroun," Taikal said. "Keep your eyes and ears open, and when we return tell us all that has passed in the camp."

"I will do that gladly," replied the singer. "My eyes and ears are seldom closed, for they are the means of song gathering." He stretched out his hand for his lute, then stopped with a surprised grunt, staring at his palm. "From where did this black come?"

In the firelight Taikal could see dark stains on Haroun's hand. "You were touching your boot."

Haroun scrubbed his clean hand on his boots. The dye came off readily in the damp of his palm. "So, I find myself cheated."

"Where did you get those boots?" Yarkut asked.

"I bought them from some Arab who had taken them in trade." He stood up, cradling his lute. "Good luck. I hope your journey will make a new song for me."

When Haroun had gone, Taikal and Yarkut began preparing for their journey. They drew trail rations, took their arms and winter clothing from the supply carts, and each saw the man he had chosen to take temporary command of his unit.

Not a yurt fire flickered in the sleeping camp as they swung into their saddles and started up, each leading a remount horse.

They galloped out of the valley and turned south, toward Tibet.

"Dabasun Nor!" Taikal shouted, pointing to a glittering lake far in the distance.

He and Yarkut were galloping side by side down the last hill, their spare mounts easily keeping up with them.

"Then we are entering the Tsaidam, of which Haroun spoke," Yarkut shouted back.

They swept down into the great salt plain on the edge of Tibet, where dry bushes struggled to live and rocks were frosted with brine-dew.

Five days of forced riding had taken them from the wooded hills of the hunt area, through the foothills of the Altai range, across the vast Gobi Desert, and beyond the hills of the Nan Shan which marked the southern border of Genghis Khan's empire. For three of the days they had rarely dismounted, not even at night, taking advantage of the freshness of their horses and the flat deserts and plains which they had crossed. They had stopped only to change to the remount horses, or to buy fresh food to eat in the saddle, saving their trail rations when they could. For the last two nights they had camped, letting the horses feast on the lush pastures of the Nan Shan. They had been glad then that they had brought their winter clothing along, for cold was gathering in the high passes.

Now they galloped through the Tsaidam toward Dabasun Nor, the easiest part of the journey behind them. The region was a desolate one of barren ground, ugly rocks, and salt-filled hollows. There was no sound except the pounding of hoofs and the wind in their ears.

The thin line of Dabasun Nor widened as their mounts kicked away the miles. "Look!" shouted Taikal. "A man!" A figure could just be made out at the shore of the lake.

"He will know where we find the caravan trail," Yarkut said.

They galloped toward the stranger, startling a flock of gulls from the shore as they neared. The stranger's horse whinnied a greeting as they approached. The man stood up after filling a leather bottle of water and spoke to them rapidly.

"Can you understand him?" Taikal asked Yarkut.

"A little. I will ask him to speak slowly." Yarkut began conversing with the man, and Taikal found that he, too, could understand. He was glad the scholars in Karakorum had taught him languages.

"We are from the empire of Genghis Khan," Yarkut said in answer to the man's questions. "Can you tell us where to find the caravan trail to Lhasa?"

"The caravan trail from the Sung Empire to Lhasa goes through dangerous areas," replied the man, remembering to speak slowly and distinctly. "I can tell you of a safer and quicker way. There is less pasture by this route, but you do not have herds with you and so may take it. South of this lake you will find a river flowing into it. Follow this river to the mountains." He then described very carefully and with much repetition the section of the route he knew. "After crossing the pass Chomburta La you must ask someone for directions, for I know not the region. Now, will you honor me by coming to my tent for refreshment? It is seldom I have guests."

"Thank you, but we must hurry on our way," said Yarkut. They let their horses drink from the lake while they filled their flasks. "What do you do in this land?" Taikal asked. "You cannot raise a herd here!"

"My herds are in the mountains where my family lives," said the man. "I gather salt to sell to passing caravans. One has only to dig a hole. When the water which seeps into it dries, salt is left behind. But soon the winter will begin in the mountains, and I must journey to Angrisha La to help my wife move our herd to warmer pastures. You must be certain to stop there. My family gladly aids travelers."

Taikal and Yarkut tightened their cinches and swung into the saddle. Their friend caught their reins. "Before you go, let me warn you of the wild dogs. In this land we use mastiffs to hunt down the musk deer, but sometimes the dogs run off and turn wild. They roam in fierce packs, and if you see any, spur your horses!"

They thanked him again and rode off along the shore of Dabasun Nor. Finding the river which flowed into it, they settled down to a hard, steady gallop. Nightfall found them still on the desolate plain. Patches of salt sparkled like hoarfrost in the moonlight.

"We will have to camp," Yarkut shouted above the pounding of hoofs.

They brought the horses down to a fast trot, both riders looking for graze. At last they found a scrubby patch of bushes. "It is better than nothing," Taikal said. They walked the horses round and round, letting them cool off before turning them out in the poor pasture.

Lighting a fire, they cooked a little rice, washing it down with the milk that the jogging of the horses had churned from the dried curds and water in their sacks. Then rolling themselves in their blankets, they went to sleep. Some time during the night Taikal was roused by the pounding of hoofs. It was the salt gatherer, he thought, going to meet the early caravans at the pass farther east.

They awoke three hours before dawn, the habit of hard riding still on them. They made a quick, cold breakfast from the slabs of dried meat they carried beneath their saddles and from the rest of the cooked rice.

"We will reach the mountains by daylight," said Taikal. "With luck we can camp tonight in the valley of which the salt gatherer spoke."

Still following the river, they galloped toward the mountains. At the first feeble light of dawn Yarkut pointed ahead. "A tent, and two horses grazing."

"And look, a horseman is coming to meet us."

As the rider approached, they saw he was only a lad. He called out a cheerful greeting, which they did not understand. Yarkut asked the boy to speak slowly.

"My master bids you a good morning and asks where you are going."

"Our respects to your master," Yarkut replied. "We are on our way to Lhasa. Does your master know the route beyond Chomburta La?"

"I will ask," replied the lad. "Do but rest your horses by the river."

"We must make haste," Taikal said. "We will ride with you to your master."

"That is not permitted," the lad said. "My master suffers a grievous affliction and will let no one see his person. I myself know not his features. But he is anxious to show his hospitality and has sent me to inquire after you."

"You are brave to serve an afflicted man," said Taikal.

"Are you not afraid of catching his disease?"

The lad gestured to the east. "He found me alone and cold in this wretched land. My former master abused me so greatly that I left the caravan before it entered the mountains some days ago. My present master travels alone, for he is a scholar and goes in odd places to study the land. Affliction or not, he has fed me and given me this horse." He hesitated, then leaned forward in his saddle. "And who knows? We may come upon lush pastures where there is need for a herdboy."

"If your master is a scholar," said Taikal, "ask if he knows of a certain animal." Carefully he described the beast which had twice charged the drive line.

The lad committed Taikal's words to memory, then rode back to the tent. The two cadets let the horses rest until the lad's return.

"My master regrets that he has never heard of such a creature as you described," said the lad. "As for the route you are taking, my master says that if you have heard this from a salt gatherer near Dabasun Nor, then you have been deceived. This route will surely lead you to your deaths."

"But why would the salt gatherer do such a thing?" Yarkut asked. "We have done him no harm."

"My master says he knows this man well, and it is not the first time he has misdirected travelers. Often pearls are found here, and the salt gatherer fears that lonely travelers will return with their companions to slay him and take his store of wealth. And so he sets them on a trail from which they can not return."

"Then must we take the caravan route?" asked Taikal. "It means losing a day of travel to go to the pass farther east."

"It is the only way," the lad assured them. "My master

says this of the trail." He carefully recited the description of
the new route. At the end he repeated a warning he had
given earlier. "You should reach the mountain called
Burkhan-Buddha before nightfall. Remember, my master
says that on no account are you to linger, but to get up on
the mountain before you make your camp. For if you remain at the bottom, the poisonous serpents will surely kill
you!"

"This must be the danger of which Haroun warned us,"
Yarkut said to Taikal. "If we ride hard, we can be on the
Burkhan-Buddha while there is still light to see by."

"My master regrets that his disfiguring ailment obliges
him to stay out of sight," the lad added. He paused, then
burst out eagerly, "Do you not need a stout lad in your
camp? I can work hard and eat little. I, too, would like to
see Lhasa."

Taikal looked at the lad's thin, pinched face and sadly
shook his head. "We travel hard and fast, for we are on an
important mission. We have little food with us."

"Perhaps," said Yarkut, "you will soon come to where a
herder is needed." They mounted and called farewell.

"Good luck on your journey," was the wistful reply.

Turning east, they spurred the horses to a hard gallop,
following the mountains. An hour before dusk they found the
caravan pass and entered the hills. At last they arrived at the
foot of a vast and craggy mountain.

"The Burkhan-Buddha," Yarkut said, gazing at the harsh
cliffs and rock-strewn path before them.

In the fading light of day Taikal could see mist gathering
on the mountain. "Let us hurry, before the fog becomes too
thick for us to see our way."

"I wish we could stay here for the night," Yarkut said.

"But we must not take the chance of losing the horses to the poisonous snakes."

They set the four horses into a line, and with Taikal at the head and Yarkut behind, started up the rugged trail. The path bent sharply back and forth across the face of the mountain, raw rock on the one hand, and a sheer drop on the other. Sometimes they came to a fairly level place branching from their trail, but it was easy to see where the caravans went, and they kept to the correct route. The path became steeper as they climbed. The horses began stumbling. Taikal paused, panting heavily in the still air while the mist clung about him like a cloak. His head was pounding and his legs were weakening.

Yarkut came up. "What is wrong?" He spoke with effort.

"Let us make camp. Surely we are beyond the snakes."

Yarkut went back to the end of the line, clumping heavily in his boots. Taikal pulled the reins of the lead horse and went on, slowly, looking for another flat place such as they had frequently passed. The mist was thickening, and the air was very still. The horses stumbled on and then began pulling back.

"Here is a gully," Taikal called, surprised at how hard it was to speak. They led the horses into the broad fissure and began gathering from the sparse bushes a few sticks for the fire.

"I can not light the wood," Taikal said after many attempts with clumsy fingers.

Yarkut took the fire striker from him, but soon he, too, confessed failure. "Why will it not light?"

Taikal felt for his blanket in the gloom of the gully. "It matters not. I am too sleepy to eat." Indeed, breathing had become a task, and simple activities were almost beyond his strength. He pulled the blanket over him, resting his aching head on his arm .

"Taikal." Yarkut stumbled back from the end of the gully. "Horses lying down." He panted from the effort of speech. "Blowing. Can not—breathe."

Taikal lay between consciousness and sleep. They should do something for the horses. But to move his dead-weight limbs seemed beyond him. Perhaps the animals would be better tomorrow.

"Taikal." Yarkut sounded as if he wanted to shake him but could not.

"All right." Heavily he sat up, blood surging into his eyes and ears. He got to his feet and staggered.

"This way," said Yarkut, making no move to go toward his friend.

Taikal blundered into the gully wall and fell. He lay there until the buzzing in his ears stopped. The mist hung above him in heavy coils. Odd that it was not cold or wet, Taikal thought. A strange mist in a strange land! It sapped the strength and confused the mind.

Summoning all his energy, Taikal put out a shaky hand to push himself upright. He felt a hard curving thing beneath it. Forgetting that he had meant to get up, he pulled the object toward him. It was white, and he could just make it out in the last dull light of day.

He dropped it suddenly. "Yarkut, I found a skull." Slowly, almost painfully, he pulled himself forward to a low mound. He tugged away a ragged blanket and gazed at the skeleton of a man in the attitude of sleep.

Someone had camped here before. And he had died in his sleep.

Was it an old man? Or a wounded man? Or a traveler such as they, who lay down in a gully on the misted mountain?

"Yarkut!" The scream was in his mind. Taikal had barely strength to force his lungs to breathe.

The mist was poisonous. He was sure of it. They had to get over the mountain at once.

Taikal pulled himself up by the rock wall of the gully. He swayed with dizziness. Yet it seemed as if it were just a little easier to breathe.

Staggering back to where he had left Yarkut, Taikal stumbled over his friend.

Fear gave him the strength he needed. Seizing Yarkut's belt, he dragged him to the gully entrance. Here the mist was not as thick. Yarkut's eyes fluttered weakly.

"Get up," Taikal commanded. "This fog is killing us."

Yarkut put out a hand. Taikal forced himself to pull on his friend's arm, and at last he had Yarkut slumped against a rock.

"Found skeleton," Taikal said laboriously. "Died sleeping. Poison mist. Get out of here."

Taikal could see Yarkut's lips move, and he leaned closer. "Horses," Yarkut said.

"Can you help?"

Yarkut pushed himself upright, swaying on his feet.

"Do not lie down," Taikal warned.

They made their way back into the dark gully. Taikal fumbled with the bridles, finally managing to get one on the first horse. Yarkut urgently tugged and kicked and at last succeeded in getting the reluctant animal to its feet. By the time Yarkut had managed to lead the first out of the gully, Taikal was ready with another. Yarkut did not return, so Taikal dealt with the second horse. After many blows it finally stood up and stumbled after Taikal, who had to fumble his way with one hand on the gully wall.

He met Yarkut who was returning. "There is a place where you can stand and breathe awhile," he said, speaking more clearly than he had for some time. He told Taikal where to find it and went after the third horse.

Taikal pulled his horse after him, his own legs becoming weaker and weaker. Farther up the caravan trail, he found the horse Yarkut had taken out. And here it did seem clearer. He could even let himself sit down for a few moments to quiet his racing heart.

He went back cautiously, for now it was completely dark. He heard the clop of hoofs and pressed against the cliff side of the trail. Yarkut passed with the third horse, and when Taikal went after the fourth he found it a little easier to work.

Resting between journeys, they brought out the saddles and supplies. The horses seemed to be in better condition than they had been in the gully.

"We can not camp here," Yarkut said, still with some effort, for the air was not free of the vapor. "We are at the edge of a cliff."

"We must cross the mountain," said Taikal. "If we go slowly, we can conserve our strength."

"But if we go quickly," said Yarkut, "the mist will not affect us as much. How many clear places like this are we likely to find?"

"Let us go then. Perhaps even here the fog will thicken soon."

With much effort they saddled two of the horses and tied their supplies on the extra mounts. Then they started up the caravan trail, leading the horses and carefully feeling their way. Taikal's headache, which had never entirely gone away, increased. Once again he found he had to concentrate on breathing. He forced his weakening legs onward.

As they struggled higher and higher, they came out of the shadows of the nearby hills and into moonlight. Still the path was not clear, for the vapor fogged the moon's brightness.

They stumbled and fell, then dragged themselves upright against the rocks. The horses often refused to go on, and sometimes one or two lay down on the path. Each time it was harder and harder to bring the beasts to their feet and make them continue. Taikal's head was spinning and he had to fight sickness. More than once he found himself standing on the very edge of a drop, looking down upon dark emptiness.

It seemed that hour on hour passed while they still struggled with the horses, with themselves, with the mountain and its deadly vapor.

The moon rose higher in the sky; the rocky trail seemed to stretch on forever. Taikal fell, and this time he let his exhausted, aching body lie. Dimly he was aware of the horses stumbling past.

Later someone roughly seized his arm. "Taikal!"

"Let me sleep," he mumbled.

"The mist thins," Yarkut said. "Up there it is much thinner."

With his friend helping him, Taikal struggled to his feet. Once again he felt the tremendous surge of blood bringing pain to his chest.

Yarkut pulled and pushed while Taikal reeled along the rocky path. Several times he fell, dragging his friend down with him. His numb body hardly felt the new scrapes and bruises. Soon Yarkut's helping hands were less steady, and he, too, was faltering. Every breath of the cloying vapor gave a new spin to the brain, an increased pounding to the blood.

Taikal sagged against a cliff. "Rest," he pleaded.

"Almost there," said Yarkut in refusal. His voice was heavier, his breathing labored, and he slumped across a boulder.

If the vapor were thinning, the moonlight would be less fuzzy. Taikal's clouded vision could detect no difference.

Why did they have to go higher up? Taikal could not remember. It was good to stay still, though the ache in his head was sending flashes of light to his closed eyes.

The salt gatherer was waiting for them, waiting with a sack of furtive pearls. No. It was the strange black and white creature, who readied his claws for them.

A few deep breaths would put an end to pain and struggle. It was not a bad way to go, for all the racing of heart and swirl of mind.

Then he remembered. He did not want to die.

And he had made his rescue hard on his friend, had exhausted Yarkut with his stumbling and falling. He waited a few moments, gathering all his resolve, for there was no strength left. Only the will to live. He fixed the will firmly, so that if the vapor again swept away the reason, he would keep on.

"Yarkut." Had he spoken at all, or had his ears gone the way of his other senses? He lurched over to his friend slumped on the rock and put out a hand. He could not feel, yet by the dim moonlight Taikal knew he was touching him. Yarkut's lips moved, but whether his friend could not speak or Taikal could not hear, he did not know. Taikal gestured upward. Slowly Yarkut pulled himself off the boulder.

Side by side they stumbled, fell, even crawled upward. Neither could help the other, but the presence of a friend in itself lent strength.

Was the moonlight getting clearer? Up, up they pushed, on legs at once sore and numb, hands without feeling holding them up on the rocky walls or nearby boulders. The burden on Taikal's heart began to lift a little.

Then there was no more path. Only boulders and rock, jagged with shadows under a bright moon. They were at the top.

The furious charge of blood through his body gradually slowed. Taikal heard the silence of the mountain, but he knew that he truly heard it, for his ears were again open. His chest heaved less and less. Now he could feel the stone beneath him where he lay. He could not remember having lain down. Near him, Yarkut sat up.

"The air is pure down there where the horses are," said Yarkut. The pause between words was not as great as on their way up. "I can not understand it. But let us go down and make camp."

They went down to where the horses were browsing on some stunted bushes. Taikal breathed the pure sweet air easily and freely.

The next day Taikal and Yarkut came upon a gigantic caravan sprawled at the foot of a mountain chain. There were hundreds of men taking their midday meal and thousands of animals grazing along the valley. As the cadets approached, they saw some of the men run for their horses, and soon a group rode out to meet them at the edge of the camp.

"Where do you go, young warriors?" asked one of the men, his eyes moving over their helmets, breastplates, and weapons.

"We travel not as warriors," answered Taikal, who by now was able to understand the Tibetans as well as Yarkut could. "We journey to Lhasa to visit the great scholars there."

"Ah, then you mean to study under the lamas," said the man.

"It is knowledge which we seek," said Yarkut. "But can you sell us a little fresh food and tell us of the trail ahead?"

"Gladly," replied the man. "Come to my tent for refreshment while we talk." They turned their horses to follow his through the camp, the other men riding with them. They dismounted before a large tent. The other men let their horses wander off, but Taikal and Yarkut tied the reins of theirs in pairs.

The group crowded into the tent, the men picking up

bowls they had put down when they had seen Taikal and Yarkut. Their host clapped his hands. A servant came and set bowls of a steaming brown liquid before them. While the cadets answered questions about their native land, the servant put a handful of meal into each bowl and worked it into a thick paste.

"But eat your *tsamba*," urged their host. "We must not let you go hungry with answering our questions."

Following the example of the men, Taikal and Yarkut scooped up the paste with their fingers and ate. "Is this not barley?" asked Yarkut. "And there is another flavor here as well."

Their host nodded. "Tea and barley. That is *tsamba*, which can be prepared at a moment's notice in all weathers or placed beneath a shirt for eating on the trail. An excellent caravan food."

"Where does this caravan go?" asked Taikal between hungry mouthfuls.

"We are two caravans," replied the host. "I help lead the one going on to Lhasa, while this man here leads the one returning from Lhasa to the Sung Empire. We met by chance in this valley."

"If you go the way we came, beware a mountain with suffocating vapors," Taikal warned the leader of the second caravan. "Try to find a way around it."

"The Burkhan-Buddha," the man said, while the others in the crowded tent quieted at the mention of the name. "There is no other way, unless you take the horseman's trail. But I have crossed the mountain many times."

"And we went over it a few days ago," said their host. "Yes, that is the hardest part of the journey. One must know when it is to be crossed."

"Then you know of it?" asked Taikal in surprise. "I thought perhaps we had taken a wrong turning somewhere."

"There are many mountains in Tibet from whose rocks issue this suffocating vapor. Nor can any fire be lighted in the strange mist," explained their host. "On the Burkhan-Buddha, which is the most famous of these mountains, the vapor is present only on the north and east sides."

"How can caravans cross it?" Yarkut asked. "We nearly died there!" As he and Taikal told of their experience on the mountain, their listeners nodded or shook their heads.

"It is fortunate you escaped," marveled their host. "The vapor is sometimes thick, as when you crossed, sometimes thinner. When it is thick, you must wait for a wind."

"Or snow," added another man.

"Rain will disperse it also," said yet another.

"The vapor is thickest when the air is calm, as it is at night and at dawn before the sun is well up."

The leader of the second caravan asked, "What made you cross at night? Did you think the other side gave better pasture for your horses?"

"It was to avoid the poisonous serpents which infest the foot of the mountain," Taikal answered. He was amazed when the men shouted with laughter. "We met someone on the trail who warned us of this," Taikal insisted. "He said that on no account must we spend the night at the foot of the Burkhan-Buddha."

"There are no nests of poisonous snakes there," said one of the men.

"Are you sure he did not mean some other mountain?" asked their host. "Perhaps he spoke of some part of the horseman's trail, which is shorter than this."

"The salt gatherer set us on the horseman's trail," said

Taikal. "But later we met a scholar." He told of the afflicted man's advice to them.

"These scholars often become confused with all the knowledge in their heads," suggested one man.

"Perhaps the lad who carried the message became confused," said the leader of the second caravan. "But when you return from Lhasa, young warriors, why do you not take the horseman's trail? It branches off the caravan route at Nag-ch'u, just south of the Tanglha Mountains. It is a rough passage for herds, but a shorter and quicker route for travelers like you."

"I can show you where the trail begins if you travel with my caravan to Lhasa," offered their host. "We would welcome your arms, for they would give us added protection against any brigands we might meet along the way."

"We would gladly travel with you," said Yarkut. "But Genghis Khan has given us only a month for our journey, and we must make all possible speed."

"Then you will want to know of the trail ahead," the host said. All the men helped to describe the route, interspersing their instructions with personal experiences on past trips and warnings about the weather.

"Will you not take *tsamba* with you?" asked the host.

Taikal shook his head. "We have dried meat beneath our saddles for trail food. But now we would like to buy fresh meat for a change of taste."

"And we will need sheep fat for the cold you told us of," added Yarkut.

"Come. Let me guide you through the camp." Their host led them out of the tent. The other men said farewell to the cadets and wished them a good journey.

Leading their horses, Taikal and Yarkut followed their

host through a maze of tents and groups of men resting after their meal or going about on errands. They stopped before a large fire where two Arabs were roasting meat. The smell was tempting, and in spite of all the *tsamba* he had eaten, Taikal felt hungry.

"Here is a camel which broke its leg coming down the mountain," their host said. "These men are cooking and selling the meat."

"It was a young, tender camel, O warriors," said the man who turned the roasting stick. "See how the fat sputters in the fire!"

Their host laughed. "It was an ill-tempered beast well advanced in age. What price for a haunch, Achmed?"

They haggled for some minutes and finally reached an agreement. Taikal paid for the meat while Yarkut tied the haunch to one of the horses.

"Do you also sell fat?" Taikal asked.

The Arab brought forth a steaming pot. "Here is a quantity just melted, young warrior. And I have spices also, to make a fine sauce for the meat."

"We do not mean to eat it," Taikal said. "I want a pot of the cold grease so we may protect our faces in the mountains."

Shaking his head and muttering about a waste of fine food, Achmed produced a pot of cold, rendered fat. Taikal bought it without haggling, for he and Yarkut had lingered long enough.

They thanked their host and mounted.

"A question," begged their host. "Are there many people at the Tsaidam pass? A merchant in the other caravan needs to replace two lads who died crossing the Bayan Kara Mountains."

"The area was deserted when we took the pass," replied Yarkut. "But remember the lad who serves the sickened scholar? Perhaps he would like employment."

"One is better than none," replied the host. "Good journey, and if something happens to delay you, remember you are welcome to join my caravan."

With many shouts of thanks and farewell Taikal and Yarkut went through the camp at a fast trot. Before them loomed Mount Shugan, sentinel of the Bayan Kara Mountains.

"We are lucky the Karakhitaian war ended early this summer," said Yarkut, as they set their horses up the rugged path. "If we had to come this way a month later, the snow might be too deep for us."

The rangy Mongol steppe horses covered in days what would take a caravan with its burdened camels and lumbering yaks weeks of slow, persistent effort.

They climbed the snow-crowned Bayan Kara Mountains, clinging to their horses' tails on the slippery path, and laughing when one of them lost his grip and fell. The rugged trail they followed held no dangers for them. Mountain and ice they knew from childhood, and under a clear blue Tibetan sky it almost seemed as if they were home again.

The barren North Plain beyond was swiftly covered by galloping hoofs. With faces and hands greased against the sharp cold of the Roof of the World, they crossed the glacier plateau of the Tanglha chain, riding on ice-choked trails beside racing hot springs.

In the warm wooded valley below, they took off their heavy sheepskin jackets and fur-lined caps and slowed their horses while looking for a cool stream to water the animals.

"Listen! Is that some animal?" warned Yarkut, glancing into the thick forest through which they rode.

Throaty growling came from the sun-dappled underbrush.

"They're coming closer," said Taikal, reaching for his bow. "Wild dogs!" he cried, catching a glimpse of a snarling muzzle and long yellow fangs through the underbrush.

Twigs snapped and bushes swayed as the pack began its rush toward them.

There was no time to nock an arrow. The horses began to rear and plunge. Taikal fought to control his reins. Using the flat of his sword, Yarkut started up the remounts, his own horse following. With his heavy bow, Taikal beat off a shaggy black-haired mastiff as the dog lunged for him savagely.

Now the other dogs leaped and snapped, racing beside the terrified horses.

Taikal felt a mastiff's hot breath as a wicked fang tore through the stiff leather of his boot. "They are still with us!" he cried to Yarkut, for the dogs had abandoned their attack on the remount horses which fled ahead of them.

"We can not gallop in these woods!" Yarkut shouted, twisting his horse through the close-set trees. He bent low over the saddle, lest he be swept off by a branch.

Snarling, the wild mastiffs lunged again and again at the horses, some of the dogs rolling as they hit the ground from Taikal's blows. Catlike, they leaped up and again flung themselves at their prey. Yarkut's mount whinnied as a claw found its mark.

"A river!" shouted Yarkut.

Taikal soon sighted a sparkle through the trees. Following Yarkut, he crashed through the underbrush and plunged into the cold water.

The river was deep and swift, and the horses fought to keep their heads above water. The cadets slipped from their saddles and held to their mount's tails. Behind, there was splashing as something else flung itself into the stream.

Taikal glanced behind, surprised and relieved that it was not the wild mastiffs which followed. The other two horses, which had scattered into the thick woods, had found the river and were now swimming across.

Ground sloped up to meet them as they approached the other side. The cadets staggered to their feet, splashing up on the bank. The two remount horses also gained dry ground and went to touch noses with their companions.

From the woods on the other side came growling and yelping. The noise faded as the mastiffs raced their unseen way.

"Why did they not follow us?" Yarkut wondered aloud. "They were anxious to tear our hearts out a moment ago."

The breeze turned, and Taikal's head went up, a musky scent tingling his nostrils. "The dogs must have caught the scent of some animal."

"The musk deer," said Yarkut. "The salt gatherer told us these dogs are trained to hunt the deer, but sometimes they run wild."

"It can not be that," said Taikal. "For surely I have smelled this same scent before. If I could only remember!"

They led their horses up the bank to level ground. Swinging into the saddle, they began to trot with the remounts following. "I do remember!" exclaimed Taikal. He sniffed the musk-scented air. "Yes, it must be the same. The cloak which was given to Bayan had been packed with spices on its journey from Cathay. Some of the odor still clung to it, and it was the same as this!"

"Do you mean the mysterious animal is attracted by this musk odor?" asked Yarkut. "Chepe Noyon was not given a cloak, and yet he was attacked."

"True, but he bore the same scent!" Taikal described the incident of the careless perfume merchant who had spilled some scent on Chepe the morning of the first beast's appearance. "I am certain it was also this musk odor. Perhaps we have found the secret of the beast's attacks!"

"Perhaps," Yarkut said. "But how is it that the musk of a Tibetan deer is found beyond the Altai Mountains?"

"That is another question for us to ask of the scholar lamas."

The route led across more mountains, but none were as high as the Tanglha chain. Grass grew thicker as the trail gradually descended. Taikal and Yarkut found trappers and hunters living in caves, then as they began following long river valleys, they met with herders living in tents. From them they purchased fresh food. Taikal could not resist drinking great quantities of milk at one of their stops.

The ground leveled off more frequently, and they saw mud houses amid tilled fields. Travel was faster for them, too, in this milder climate and smoother terrain. Now they began passing through regular settlements. They crossed the vast rich plain of Pampu, where it was as warm as summer and fruit hung heavily on the trees.

Struggling over a last rugged mountain, they saw the slope fall away to a vast pleasant valley watered by the Tsangpo. Hundreds of white houses with flat red roofs clustered in a bend of the river. The city was circled by a belt of green parks.

"Lhasa!"

Then Yarkut pointed to a low mountain on the rim of the

city. Nestled in its rocky folds was the largest building they had ever seen in their lives. The windows seemed to number thousands and the flat red roofs hundreds. The huge white walls threw their reflections into a crystal lake at the lamasery's feet. "The Potala," Yarkut said.

They went down the mountain and entered the magnificent city.

The babble of voices and the rush of people in the crowded streets confused and frightened the steppe horses. Taikal and Yarkut had to put halters on the extra mounts, then go on foot, leading all four horses.

"Let us go to the bazaar for something to eat," Taikal suggested.

Following directions a passer-by gave them, they found the crowded Bar Kor. This bazaar in the center of the city wound its zigzag street through tall whitewashed mud buildings. Shops were next to houses, which were squeezed shoulder to shoulder with Buddhist academies and temples.

"I see a shop selling fruit," said Yarkut.

They edged their horses through the crowd of gaily dressed women, running children, slow-paced shaven-headed lamas in their red robes, and officials trotting by on horses.

They bought fruit and began eating it at once. "How can we reach the Potala?" Taikal asked as he paid the shopkeeper.

"That is easy enough," replied the Tibetan, and he told them the way through the winding streets of the city. "But if you hope to see the Pandit Ch'en Po, the greatest of the scholars, you must depart in disappointment. The Pandit Ch'en Po is busy with many tasks and has little time for visitors."

"If the Pandit is the wisest lama in the Potala," replied

Yarkut, "then it is to him we will put our questions."

Mounting, they followed the directions the shopkeeper had given them. The horses were becoming accustomed to the bustle of the city and only shied once when a laden yak pressed too close.

On the other side of Lhasa they passed through a great park of ponds and trees. Following the shore of the crystal lake, they finally stood before the massive stone lamasery of a thousand windows and a hundred roofs. The building was on several different levels, rambling over the cliffs and steep slopes.

"Do you think we can get the horses up?" Yarkut asked, studying the rock-hewn stairway up the mountain to the entrance.

"It is a long way to walk," said Taikal. "But I think the horses will slip on the steep stairs, and the ground on either side is sharp with rocks."

They tied the horses two by two, looping the reins over a convenient rock.

It was a long way to the top, and Taikal's legs ached when they reached the main entrance, double doors hewn of massive wood and ornamented with gold. Just then one of the great doors opened, and a little boy hardly more than nine years old stepped out. There was a large wooden bowl strapped to his shoulder and his head was shaven. He wore the red robes of the lama.

When he saw the two cadets, bristling with weapons, he stopped and blinked his large black eyes. At Taikal's greeting he bowed deeply.

"We have come to see the Pandit Ch'en Po, little one," said Taikal. "Will you not go and tell him we are here?"

The boy bowed again and shyly stepped back through the door. They waited only a few minutes before he reappeared, accompanied by a lama. The man patted the boy on his shaven head. "Run along, Kyarwong." The boy obediently clambered down the long stone steps. "Kyarwong goes to beg alms for Buddha," the lama explained. "You wish to see the Pandit Ch'en Po? I am afraid that is not possible."

"We have traveled for fourteen days from the Altai Mountains," Taikal said. "Genghis Khan has given us permission for this trip so we may ask questions of the greatest of all scholars."

"They are short questions, easily answered," Yarkut added.

"Ah, you are warriors of Genghis Khan!" exclaimed the lama. "Even here we have heard of this man's empire. Surely the Pandit Ch'en Po will want to see you. Enter, then. I will send boys to take care of your horses."

They followed the lama into a great stone hall, bare except for rows of golden images along the walls. A few lamps flickered feebly in the gloom. They traced winding corridors and steep narrow stairs until they stood before an ivory gate. "Remain here." The lama bowed and disappeared.

Soon the ivory gate was opened by two solemn-eyed boys the same age as little Kyarwong. "Enter, O travelers," they chanted together.

Taikal and Yarkut stepped through the ivory gate. They found themselves in a great hall, its polished stone floor reflecting the lights of the many lamps placed along the walls and hanging from the high ceiling. A strip of red carpet led to a golden throne, on which sat the Pandit Ch'en Po, the greatest of the scholars.

He wore the simple robes of the other lamas, but a long pointed red cap covered his shaven head.

They approached him and bowed deeply. From Yarkut's tongue flowed a beautifully phrased greeting, and Taikal envied his friend's quickness with words. Feeling he, too, should say something, Taikal told the Pandit Ch'en Po their names and where they were from.

"You have some questions to ask me," said the Pandit. "And I, too, seek information and would have you tell me of Genghis Khan. But first, let us take tea." He clapped his hands, and the two boy lamas instantly appeared with bowls and a stone pitcher. One placed cushions on the floor for the visitors to sit upon, and the other poured a thick liquid into the bowls and served them.

"You Mongols do not know our tea," remarked the Pandit Ch'en Po as he sipped from his steaming bowl. "We take certain dried leaves and steep them in hot water, to which we add salt and butter. It is very delicious. We Tibetans prize tea so highly that often pressed bricks of it are used as barter tokens. Now tell me of the land of Genghis Khan. Are there lamas among you?"

"Indeed, and they are welcome," said Taikal between sips of the hot rich liquid. "Genghis Khan prizes scholars as much as you do your tea." He and Yarkut then answered many questions about their native land, its customs, and history.

The Pandit Ch'en Po listened attentively, eagerly absorbing this new knowledge. At last he was satisfied. "Now tell me what brings you here."

"In hunting it is our custom to form a line of horsemen and drive the animals ahead until we encircle them," explained Taikal. "One day a mysterious animal appeared." Taikal told of the two beasts attacking the line, one killing a soldier. "Our scholars could tell us nothing about this creature or why it charged so savagely. But a lute-singer told us that such an animal is kept here in the Potala. So we have traveled a great distance to learn of this creature." Careful to leave nothing out, Taikal described the black and white beast.

"You speak of an animal with many names," said the Pandit. "It is the giant panda, or niyalya-ponga, also known as the beishung. Some remote mountain people even call it the ye-ti and claim it is dangerous. So rarely is the creature seen that many legends have sprung up concerning it. These tales have traveled beyond the range of the animal, and it seems that sometimes other rare creatures have been given some of these names." He leaned forward. "But is it curiosity alone which drove you to take this long, terrible journey in so little time?"

Yarkut took up the tale. "There is a man among us who claims he is a spirit-talker, a magician. He says this animal is a spirit and that he has control over it. Already he has many foolish men believing him."

"But if we can show that the animal, though strange to us, is common elsewhere," added Taikal, "then this trouble-maker will be without followers."

The Pandit Ch'en Po nodded thoughtfully. "Perhaps you would like to see the animal as I tell you of its habits." He rose from the golden throne.

Taikal and Yarkut eagerly followed the Pandit through the ivory gate. Their guide led them through narrow passages, lighted only by smoking lamps. Once they came out on a gallery overlooking an enclosed garden which was crowded with groups of young lamas. "This is our school," the Pandit Ch'en Po explained. "Here the novices learn the wise words of the Buddha. As lamas, they will often have to convince stubborn men to turn away from evil."

"It is said they also learn all the languages of the world," said Yarkut.

"All the important languages," the Pandit Ch'en Po corrected. "We do not bother with the strange tongues of the barbaric peoples living in the Far West, in Europe. They know little of art, science, and trade and so are unimportant in world affairs."

The Pandit nodded toward a group of debating students. "The scholars keep all our records, translate important writings into our language, and compose the hymns we chant three times a day. But there are other tasks besides clerical ones. Some of our young lamas will go out among the people, teaching them the Good Way. Other lamas do their good work by keeping our cattle and sheep or by raising grain to distribute among the poor."

Now Taikal understood even more clearly the difference between such charlatans as Basukor and truly religious men like the Pandit Ch'en Po. "Then it is you who rules this country?" he asked.

The Pandit Ch'en Po shook his head. "I lead only the people's hearts and minds if they choose to live the Good Way. Once Tibet was strong with mighty kings, but they began quarreling and fighting among themselves and cared not for the people. Today there are only a few petty chieftains left. And so Tibetans turn for guidance to the lamas."

"Do you have an army?" Yarkut asked. "We saw no soldiers on the way."

"There is no army," the Pandit said. "The mountains keep us safe from invasion by other lands. And most of our people follow the Good Way—a code of conduct laid down by the Buddha—so there is little quarreling among them. It is true that caravans are sometimes attacked by brigands, but this means only that we lamas have not yet finished our work."

They left the gallery and followed the Pandit Ch'en Po through more dark, winding corridors. The way took them up and down numerous steps, and finally they paused before a stout wooden door. At a gesture from the Pandit, Taikal and Yarkut pulled open the heavy portal. The Pandit took one of the lamps from the wall of the corridor and entered. From the first lamp he lighted others in the room. "Here is the giant panda," said the scholar. He brought one of the lamps close to a barred cage. The flickering light danced over black and white fur.

Taikal stepped close and studied the animal. "Yes, this is the same beast which attacked the drive line."

The panda blinked sleepily, then lazily stretched itself. It pushed its head against the bars near Taikal and opened its mouth. Quickly Taikal pulled back.

"It will not harm you," the Pandit said, putting his hand out to let the animal lick it. "The giant panda is a shy creature and will fight only when at bay."

"Then is there nothing which would drive it into a savage attack?" Taikal persisted. "No color, or sound, or scent?"

"None that we know of," the Pandit Ch'en Po replied. "This animal was captured by lamas after we received reports from eastern Tibet of a strange creature which roamed dense mountain forests during the night. The panda is also found in southwestern Cathay, where Tibet's border meets that of the Sung Empire. Many of the local people circulated terrifying rumors of the ye-ti. They were certain it had supernatural powers and meant to kill any human."

"That is what the magician Basukor tells our people," Yarkut said.

"But our studies show that the animal is really harmless," explained the Pandit. "It lives on bamboo shoots, berries, roots, or even small animals. It does have an enormous appetite, however, and its teeth show that in past ages the panda was principally an eater of flesh. Its claws are powerful, and the animal is limber enough to climb trees, where it sometimes sleeps."

"But why does it have both black and white fur?" Taikal asked. "Surely it finds it hard to go unnoticed both day and night."

"The panda lives high in the forested mountains," reminded the Pandit Ch'en Po. "There, whether it is day or night, white snow, black rock, and tree shadows make an excellent background for the animal."

Taikal thrust a booted foot through the bars and prodded the panda. Though it growled frighteningly, the animal merely moved away. "There must be something which will cause the beast to attack a line of horsemen," Taikal insisted.

"Can we not ask the Pandit Ch'en Po to let the creature smell the musk?" Yarkut suggested.

"Do you mean the musk deer?" asked the Pandit. "What does this scent mean to you?"

Taikal explained his identifying the scent and his hope that this was the secret of the panda's vicious attacks.

The Pandit nodded. "Yes, the dogs you saw were after the deer. This musk makes a rare and valuable perfume. When the deer comes into musk, which happens at every moon, the scent fills the air for miles around. You think that this scent drives the panda into an attacking rage? We can but try it." The Pandit Ch'en Po stepped into the passage and struck a gong. A boy lama soon appeared and was sent for a vial of musk scent.

"We use this scent in our services, along with other spices and incense," the Pandit explained as he pulled the stopper from the ivory vial. A heavy musky odor coiled through the room.

"That is the same scent," Taikal said.

They kept their eyes on the panda as the scholar approached the cage with the ivory vial.

The black and white beast's nose twitched, and it began to paw its muzzle. The mouth opened, showing the great yellow teeth. Chest muscles rippled.

And then the panda sneezed.

The Pandit Ch'en Po stoppered the vial.

"You must have been mistaken," he said.

A deep wail of horns the next morning awoke Taikal and
Yarkut in the simple lama's cell they had been given. Spring-
ing up from their beds of hay, they took turns washing in
the large wooden bowl a boy lama had brought them the
night before, along with their meal. The Pandit Ch'en Po
had excused Taikal and Yarkut from the common supper,
for he had seen they were tired. But they knew he would
expect them to join the lamas in the great hall for the first
meal of the day.

They had just finished making ready when the student
lama appeared at the doorway. "The Pandit Ch'en Po asks
you to join him in breakfast."

"We will be happy to," replied Yarkut with a gravity that
equaled the young lama's.

Their guide led them through winding corridors to the
same ivory-gated hall where they had met the Pandit the day
before. He was on his golden throne, and before him sat
rows and rows of red-robed, shaven-headed lamas of various
ages, taking up all the room on the polished stone floor.

The voices of the lamas rose and fell together, now softer,
now louder. The sound was like the rise and fall of the desert
wind. Awed by the chanting, Taikal and Yarkut stood near
the ivory gate, not daring to intrude. Now and then the
voices paused, and the lamas clapped their hands sharply
before continuing their chant.

"The clapping marks the ends of the verses," the youthful lama explained in a hush.

When the desert wind of voices had died away, the cadets were led before the golden throne and seated upon cushions. With his own hands the Pandit Ch'en Po poured tea into bowls, dropped into each a handful of barley, and handed this *tsamba* to his visitors. He gave them other bowls of the thick, buttery tea to drink. Behind them as they ate, Taikal heard the lamas being served by the younger students.

"I have given much thought to the strange behavior of the pandas you met during Genghis Khan's hunt drive," said the Pandit Ch'en Po, sipping his tea. "Once when traveling to the lamasery Ta-Lung in the valley of Phon-Po, I saw a man in a yellow cloak attacked and slain by a yak for no apparent reason. Upon inquiring, I learned that this yak had been owned by a man who had abused it. This man always wore a vest of yellow silk, and so the yak had learned to fear and hate the color."

Taikal listened politely, though he could not see what this had to do with the panda.

"In my youth," continued the Pandit, "I lived near a man who had trained his horse to fall to its knees whenever its master clucked his tongue. I rode with this man to market one day, and as we crossed a shallow river, some birds started up and began clucking. The horse at once fell to its knees, spilling its master into the river."

Yarkut laughed, but Taikal was beginning to understand what the Pandit was saying. "The mastiffs trained to hunt the musk deer," said Taikal, "are probably rewarded with some of the meat. That is why, when they run wild, the scent of musk makes them attack."

The Pandit Ch'en Po nodded. "An animal can learn to do

things that are not in its nature. It can be taught through abuse, or kindness, and through the giving and withholding of food."

"The panda, you said, has a huge appetite," Yarkut recalled.

"An animal," continued the Pandit, "can be trained to respond to a sight, a sound, or a scent."

"The scent of the musk deer carries for miles," Taikal said.

"Do you mean, then," asked Yarkut, "that someone has trained these pandas to attack when it smells the musk of the Tibetan deer?"

"That could have been done," said the Pandit. "But this would mean that there are persons of evil among you."

"They will be sought out," Taikal replied with determination. "Can you tell us, Pandit Ch'en Po, if pandas have been captured by traders and sent north of Tibet?"

The Pandit shook his head. "You must ask the tradesmen of Lhasa. As they hear all the news of the caravan trails, they could tell you." The Pandit put aside his bowl of *tsamba*. From his sleeve he drew a scroll of parchment with a golden seal. "Here is a letter to your Khan, describing the panda and its habits. I am sorry I can not also put in it the solution to your problem."

Murmuring thanks, Taikal took the scroll. "I wonder if I might press your hospitality yet further, Pandit Ch'en Po," he said. At a nod from the great scholar, Taikal asked, "May I take with me the ivory vial of the musk scent? In this way I can make certain whether this is truly the odor which caused the pandas to attack the drive line."

"I will send it to you in time for your departure," the Pandit replied. The great hall echoed with the increasing restlessness of the lamas, for breakfast was drawing to a close. "You are welcome to stay as long as you wish," said the Pandit. "Yet you told me you had to hasten homeward. Student lamas are even now assembling supplies for you."

The Pandit Ch'en Po stood up. Taikal could hear the other lamas getting to their feet. Their youthful guide appeared at Yarkut's elbow. "One thing more," said the Pandit. "I am sending our panda to Genghis Khan as a gift." He waved aside their surprised exclamations. "I do this so he may continue to look upon the Buddhist lamas with favor and know that we are a peaceful country."

"Is it at all possible for the panda to reach Karakorum within a month?" Yarkut asked with almost rude haste. "At that time we will hold the festival which marks the end of the hunt. It would be fitting for your gift to arrive then, so that a multitude of people may behold it."

"It would be difficult," the Pandit replied. "We have no carts in our country, for the passes are narrow and rocky." He thought for a moment. "Yet a small party, by changing animals at every stop, and hastening day and night over good ground, could travel more quickly than a larger caravan."

"There are carts to be had beyond the Tsaidam," Taikal said. "The people between Tibet and the Khan's empire are friendly to us. A post rider could be sent to them, asking that they give carts and fresh animals, so the party need not stop long to rest during that part of the journey."

The Pandit Ch'en Po nodded decisively. "It will be done then. We have men who, like you, are not afraid of a hard journey."

Their thanks were shortened by the nervous cough of the boy lama near them. Taikal and Yarkut quickly bowed and turned aside. The other lamas now came forward in small groups, bowing deeply to the Pandit Ch'en Po, then hurrying off to their classes.

"Why were you anxious that the panda arrive in time for the hunt festival?" Taikal asked Yarkut, as they hurried through the winding stone corridors after their young guide.

"So that the Khan can prove to everyone in the hunt that the panda is a real animal, not a spirit," Yarkut replied. "That would be harder to do after the army has disbanded for the winter, to go home with their wild tales. But why did you want the ivory vial of musk scent? It will not cause the animal to go into a rage as we had thought."

"The scent must have something to do with the mysterious attacks," Taikal said. "If we bring some back, we might find it useful in proving someone's guilt."

At their cell a boy lama was ready to carry their sacks of *tsamba*, tea leaves, and thinly shaved dried meat. Taikal and Yarkut rolled up their blankets and other equipment, making neat bundles to tie on the extra horses. Another student lama appeared briefly and handed Taikal the ivory vial of musk scent. The cadets put on their armor and then followed their guide through the winding corridors and down the long stone steps outside.

Lhasa was a red and white jewel in the morning sun. Two other boys had brought up their horses, and the students helped tie on the provisions. Then, with shouts and cheers, the boys bade farewell.

Taikal and Yarkut skirted the crystal lake, each leading one of the remounts. "Shall we question the merchants about pandas being sent out of Tibet?" asked Yarkut as they entered the crowded city.

"Yes, for who knows but what we may hear a familiar name?"

Passers-by gave them the names of three men known to deal with animals other than livestock. The shop of the first man was loud with the chirps and whistles of monkeys, squirrels, cormorants and singing birds, and the furious yapping of small Cathayan dogs.

"There was one man I know of who once took a live snow leopard from the northern mountains," the merchant said in answer to their questions. "He sold it to a prince in the Hind country south of us. It is said he captured other wild animals in the eastern mountains."

"Where may we find this man?" Taikal asked.

"Oh, he is still in the Hind country," replied the merchant. "The prince made him his chief hunter. But while in Lhasa he stayed with a friend of mine who may be able to tell you more." He gave a name and directions.

The merchant's friend was a goldsmith. He paused in his work to invite his visitors for tea, for he seemed to welcome company. "Yes, I remember the man well," the goldsmith said, after his wife had set bowls of tea before them. "He was certain the snow leopard would bring him wealth, and so it did. He troubled to send me word of his new station. I took him into my house because I was the only man not afraid of his leopard. We talked for many hours, for he was a man of adventure."

Between sips of tea the goldsmith related the adventurer's life and exploits. Finally he said the words Taikal had hoped to hear. "He even captured a mythical beast, or rather, three of these beishungs, as the Cathayans call them," said the goldsmith. "And though some say he was nothing but a braggart, I believe him still." In detail he described the hardships of the man's journey, the stalking, and finally the capture of the black and white beasts. "He took them to Gu-Balik, the chief city of Kara Khitai," said the goldsmith. "But Gutchluk did not reward him the way he had hoped, and so he went after a snow leopard."

"When did this happen?" Taikal asked.

"It was more than a year ago," replied the goldsmith. "Some said the whole story was untrue, but I still believe the bei-shung is a real animal."

"It is real," said Yarkut. "We have seen it in the Potala."

"Aha! What did I tell you? I believed it all along!" This man, who had no adventures of his own to tell, was immensely pleased that his borrowed tale had proven true.

Taikal was conscious of the passing time, but he had one more question. "I am told Tibetans take the trouble to train dogs to hunt down the musk deer. Where, then, is the musk sent?"

"To all parts of the world!" The goldsmith gestured broadly. "To the great cities of Kharesmia, to Persia, to the Kin and Sung Empires of Cathay."

"And to Kara Khitai?" asked Yarkut.

"That, too," said the goldsmith. "Ah, the stories I could tell of great deer hunts and of dogs which have turned wild."

"I wish we might hear them," said Taikal. "But we can not stay longer."

Thanking the companionable goldsmith for his hospitality, Taikal and Yarkut led their horses through the crowded Bar Kor.

"It will be many days before we reach the hunt drive," Yarkut said. "Let us have a last taste of fresh fruit before our journey."

They began looking for a fruit stall, making their way between children running errands, women doing their marketing, yaks trudging under their burdens, and dogs running freely everywhere.

A horseman trotted up from behind, leading another mount. Taikal moved his horses aside to let the man pass.

"There is a shop over there," Yarkut said, pointing.

As Taikal turned to look, he caught a glimpse of the flank of the passing horse. The brilliant sun showed a pattern of scars on the rump. Uttering a cry, Taikal threw his reins to Yarkut and swiftly began shouldering his way through the crowd after the horseman.

He could not see the man, but he went toward the clopping of hoofs. Reaching the sound, he saw a lama pacing on his horse. There was again the sound of hoofs, and Taikal pushed his way after it, only to find a merchant leading a string of pack horses.

There was nothing around Taikal but unknown faces and a street crowded with strange buildings. Nowhere was there a horse with the brand he sought. Many dark alleyways led off from this main street. The horseman could have gone down any one of them. Taikal wondered, as he made his way back to Yarkut, if the man had heard his startled exclamation.

"What were you after?" Yarkut asked. "I did not know if you wanted me to follow you."

"I thought I could find him alone," Taikal said. "We should have chased him on our horses and returned later for the two remounts. I saw," he explained, "a rider pass us, leading a horse bearing the brand of Genghis Khan."

"You must have been mistaken," said Yarkut. "We have all four army horses with us, each with the Khan's brand."

"I did not think of stealing," said Taikal. "But perhaps someone followed us to Lhasa. I wanted to see who it was."

"You forget that Gutchluk received some of our horses as part of Jiemdad's ransom," said Yarkut.

"That is true," Taikal admitted. "Each could have been traded many times over so that one or two might appear in Lhasa."

They bought quantities of fruit, stuffing it in their rolled blankets and sheepskins, and then made their way out of the glittering red and white city.

They followed the caravan trail north, the ground rising steeper with each passing day. At the village of Nag-ch'u they purchased fresh meat and were set upon the horseman's trail across the Tanglha chain. Even in the few days since their first crossing, the mountains had grown colder, the snow deeper.

They were following the rough track which wound down the Tanglha's northern side well below the snow line when Yarkut uttered a cry and flung up his arm. Far above them Taikal saw a cloud of dust moving down the mountain in what seemed to be majestic silence. "A slide! A slide!" Yarkut shouted, pulling his horse to the side of the trail.

The remounts were between them. Taikal brought up his horse and, with the ends of his reins, slapped hard on the rump nearest him. Yarkut had prodded the other horse past him, and now he rode after it, whipping the ends of his reins. Taikal followed, driving his own remount before him. Now he could hear the rumbling of the slide. It thundered louder and even covered the frantic hoofbeats of the racing horses. Yarkut shouted something, but Taikal could not hear the words.

The trail swerved dangerously. They had to slow down, while behind them the slide roared and rocks trembled under the impact of other rocks. Dirt rained upon them. Without looking back, they drove onward.

Stones, flung high by the slide, thudded near the horses. Taikal's mount reared and pawed the air on the narrow, rocky trail. He fought its head down while stones pelted on his helmet and breastplates, and finally he got his mount to follow the other horses.

At a wide place in the trail they stopped and looked back. Masses of earth and stone still thundered downward. Dust streamed up like plumes from the avalanche roaring past the trail, sweeping the rocky road from the face of the mountain. Boulders hitting an obstruction sprang high in the air, arching into the valley below. Taikal felt the earth tremble from the pounding of rock. The thunder gradually died away; the avalanche slowed, and then, as abruptly as it had started, there was no sound, no movement.

Taikal found his legs trembling from the near disaster. "Let us walk the horses for a while to calm them," he suggested.

There were no more landslides, but Taikal and Yarkut were glad when they left the Tanglha range behind a day later. Now on the great North Plain, they could make better time. "Perhaps we can ride day and night for a while," Yarkut suggested hopefully.

Taikal agreed, but that night, riding on top of the steep bank of a river that had cut its way deep into the plain, they were hailed by a lone traveler.

"Where is he?" asked Taikal, peering into the dark, for the moon had not yet risen.

"I can make out a tent ahead of us," Yarkut said.

As they approached, Taikal could see the tent too. He heard the nickering of strange horses. A figure came toward them as they stopped their horses.

"Young men, can I not kindle a fire and offer you refreshment?" the man asked in Arabic. His head was swathed against the cold, and Taikal could see only the man's eyes in the starlight.

"Your hospitality is welcome," replied Yarkut in the Arab tongue. "But we must deny ourselves comfort in order to make haste."

"You are not in trouble, are you?" asked Taikal, remembering how the man had cried out to them.

"Alas, I am in fear for my life!" replied the man. "I am a merchant on my way to purchase goods for trade. I carry with me gold and silver. But there are brigands in the neighborhood. I saw them several times today. I am certain they mean to kill me."

"We have seen no brigands," said Yarkut.

"I am traveling from the west," replied the merchant, "and you come from the south. Tomorrow I will hasten away from this ill-favored region, but tonight my horses are too tired to continue. And so I beg, young warriors, that you stay the night and protect me."

"What do you think?" Yarkut asked Taikal in Mongol.

"It is hard to refuse such an appeal," Taikal replied. "And if our horses are well rested, we can make up the time later."

In Arabic, Taikal said they would camp there for the night.

The Arab was overjoyed. Saying he would fetch them bowls of food, he hurried off to his dark tent. Taikal and Yarkut unsaddled their horses.

"If there are brigands, the Arab has chosen his camp well,"

said Yarkut. "No robbers can come up on the river side at least, for the bank is high and steep, like a cliff."

They tied the horses in pairs by their halters and left them grazing. The Arab came with bowls of *tsamba*, and again thanking them and Allah, left them to their rest.

"Sleep soundly," Taikal advised while they ate. "I do not believe there are brigands about. The Arab is merely anxious because of carrying so much money."

"There are no caravans in this area which would attract robbers," Yarkut agreed. "But our horses will be the fresher for the next two days' riding."

They rolled themselves in their blankets near the cliff and soon fell asleep.

Taikal was sleeping soundly, but, as always, one part of his brain measured the sounds of the night. The occasional noises from the horses passed through his unconscious without alarm, as did the sighing of the wind through the grass. But then, later, there was a strange step and the breathing of a human.

Taikal sprang awake, tearing his blankets aside, clawing for his sword. "Yarkut!" A blade swished near him in a vicious stroke. A shadow bulked against the stars. It came forward, and the sword blade glinted.

The night rang with the smash of steel as Taikal met the sword with his own.

Yarkut leaped up, his blade singing as he whipped it toward the brigand. There was a faint thud; the man grunted and staggered. Taikal got to his feet, sword poised.

The robber went into a crouch, his sword hand sagging.

"Kindle a light," Taikal said. "And bring rope to bind him."

Yarkut began turning away, and then the man uncoiled,

lunging forward, driving his sword ahead of him. Yarkut was off balance. Taikal leaped forward and fell to his knees, his sword held out before him.

He felt the scrape of the robber's sword as it swept over the lacquered armor on his back. Then there was a shock through his own weapon. The brigand screamed and reared back, ripping the sword from Taikal's grip. The robber clawed, found the blade, and with desperate strength jerked Taikal's sword from his body.

Yarkut came toward him warily, his weapon ready.

The robber sobbed and staggered close to the cliff. He stumbled backward and then disappeared. A long wail echoed through the night, and then there was silence. The moon began to rise.

"So the Arab was right," said Yarkut. "Let us see if harm has come to him."

They ran to his tent and found it empty. "I will see if he took his horses away," said Yarkut.

Taikal searched through the tall grass but did not come upon the Arab's body. Yarkut returned. "Our horses are there, and so are two others with strange markings. Whether both are the Arab's or one belonged to the robber, I know not."

"We would have heard hoofs if either the Arab or the brigand used a horse," said Taikal. "The robber must have walked a long way. Both these horses are surely the Arab's, and so I fear our merchant friend is dead."

"But there is no body!"

"The robber could have thrown it over the cliff," said Taikal.

The moon was higher now, and they walked to the edge, peering down to the river below.

"I see nothing," said Yarkut. "Not even the brigand. Wait—is that a sword down there?"

"Yes, and I see its scabbard too. Over there, by the rocks. And look! Is that not a boot? It must have come off when the robber reached the bottom."

"The brigand himself must have struck the rocks and fallen into the river," said Taikal. "There is no sign of him, and the current seems swift."

They could find no trace of the Arab, and the bank was too high and steep for them to attempt climbing down to the river. "But surely we would see some garment or other possession on the rocks if the robber had flung him down the cliff," said Yarkut. "It is as if the Arab simply disappeared."

"Perhaps he awakened and had to leave his tent and then noticed the brigand creeping up," suggested Taikal. "In fright the Arab probably slipped away and will return tomorrow."

"There is little use in guarding an empty tent," said Yarkut. "Let us be on our way."

"What of the merchant's gold and silver?" asked Taikal. "We can not leave it here for anyone to take."

"There do not seem to be many travelers along this road," said Yarkut. "But let us bury the man's treasure. We can leave a note to him among his things, in the event that he does return."

They went back to the tent and fumbled through the Arab's blankets. "Surely it is here," Yarkut said. "The man could hardly creep away with bags of jingling coins. And the robber could not have had the money on him for the same reason."

They brought the contents of the tent out into the moonlight. Besides blankets and some extra clothing, there were two sacks of barley, another of dried fruit, and two or three bowls. Saddle, packrack, baskets, and bridles completed the merchant's traveling equipment.

"Strange," muttered Taikal. "Surely he would not have lied about having money."

Yarkut was running his hands through the barley. "Here is something." He pulled a small leather bag out of the grain sack. Opening it, he spilled into his hand tiny spheres which glowed softly, like little moons, in the light of their big brother.

"Pearls," said Taikal. "There was no Arab and no robber. Yarkut, we have been followed."

"The Arab merchant who besought our help and the brigand who tried to kill us were the same man," said Taikal.

"Come, let us build a fire and have some refreshment while we talk," said Yarkut. He tied the bag of pearls and fastened it to his belt. Taikal began gathering fuel.

Soon they sat before a cheerful blaze, sipping bowls of the Tibetan herb drink and eating *tsamba*.

"Our follower has played many parts," said Taikal. "His first disguise was that of a scholar disfigured by illness so that he could not meet us face to face."

Yarkut nodded. "He claimed he knew the salt gatherer of the Tsaidam, yet in truth he was a stranger to the region because he did not warn us of the Burkhan-Buddha. Wait a moment!" Yarkut set down his bowl of *tsamba*. "He did know of the poison vapor, for it is famous among Tibetans. Because of this danger, the salt gatherer set us on the horseman's route. It was the 'scholar' who insisted we go the way of the caravan trail, and he made certain we would spend the night on the mountain, when the air was sure to be still and the vapor dense." He paused in thought. "But how did the 'scholar' get ahead of us?"

"The night before we met him, I was roused by hoofbeats," Taikal said. "I thought it was the salt gatherer, but now we know it was our follower. He probably learned our route from the Tibetan at Dabasun Nor."

"He could have followed us all the way from the drive line," Yarkut added. "People would be willing to say that we passed their way if he told them he was a friend bearing urgent news."

"The salt gatherer no doubt warned him of the Burkhan-Buddha," Taikal said. "We would have learned of it, too, had we insisted on knowing what the danger of the caravan trail was. It must have been then that our enemy formed his plan to misdirect us."

Yarkut nodded. "He would need the salt gatherer's tent for his deception. Perhaps it was in forcing the Tibetan to pack it on his horse that our enemy came across the sack of pearls. Then he must have taken the Tibetan's horse, so that he could not ride for help. It must have been this horse that the serving lad rode, or surely we would have noticed it was an army horse, as you recognized the one in Lhasa. But how did our follower know that he would meet up with a wandering boy?"

"That was his stroke of fortune," Taikal said. "He might have planned to approach us as he did tonight, with head wrapped against cold winds. But when he discovered the boy, his plan became easier."

"The lad was a stranger in the region," Yarkut said, "and so would not question the directions his master gave us." He thought for a moment. "It might be that our follower later went to the caravan pass and waited for someone to come through and say they had found two dead young warriors on the Burkhan-Buddha. And surely the caravan we met told the story of how we believed in poisonous snakes at the foot of the mountain."

"He knew then we were still alive and on our way to

Lhasa to ask about the black and white beast," Taikal said. "Remember, we had asked if he knew of the animal. He must have taken the horseman's trail and then driven himself to make up the time he had lost."

"And his serving lad no doubt accepted employment in the caravan," Yarkut said. "Probably our follower even gave him the salt gatherer's horse for payment, glad to be rid of the lad so he could travel faster alone. He still had his own two horses for speed."

"Could he have known we saw the Pandit Ch'en Po in the Potala?" asked Taikal. "Lhasa is large, and surely he could not hope to meet the few people who gave us directions."

"I know not," said Yarkut. "But if he tarried in Lhasa's Bar Kor, he certainly caught a glimpse of us. Perhaps he saw our horses outside the goldsmith's shop."

Taikal nodded. "He could have questioned the goldsmith after we left. It would be easy to contrive some excuse to make the artisan eager to tell all about our visit. We had just told the goldsmith of the beishung in the Potala. The man was so excited by this proof of his adventurer's truth that no doubt he told our follower of it."

"I remember we also asked the goldsmith about the musk of the Tibetan deer," added Yarkut.

"And then our follower realized we had stumbled upon one of his secrets. He must have wanted desperately to slay us. Of course, by now we knew better than to take the caravan trail, so he could ride ahead, confident of meeting us on the horseman's route."

"The landslide," said Yarkut thoughtfully. "Do you think it was started by our follower?"

"Perhaps, but it must have been on impulse," said Taikal. "He seems to have planned to pass as a helpless merchant, for you say that his two horses are not army mounts."

Yarkut nodded. "It would have been easy for him to ride off the trail before it splits into the two routes at Nag-ch'u. In some little village he could have traded his own horses for two local mounts, then continued, disguised as a merchant in search of trade goods."

"As an Arab unused to this climate, he kept his face swathed against the cold," Taikal said. "When we were asleep, he crept up to kill us. Luckily we were quicker."

"It seems a great deal of trouble," said Yarkut. "Why did he not use his bow any time along the trail? As the 'robber' fell, I saw he wore a quiver of arrows."

"One of us surely would have escaped and later hunted him down," replied Taikal. "I do not think he meant to kill us until he learned we were interested in the panda. Up to the time he sent his serving lad to us, he probably wanted only to know our plans. He could have invented any sort of tale to suit the circumstances. He chose to let the convenient mountain be the cause of our deaths. When it failed, he had to continue following us. The landslide did not kill us either, and so he had to risk awakening one of us while he slew the other. He failed in that too."

"Taikal, our wits were not sharp when we met this spurious Arab tonight, for now I recall many slips in his tale," said Yarkut. "The moon was not yet risen, and it was so dark we could barely make out his figure. How then did he know we were 'young men' and 'warriors'? And the bend in this river has turned our trail westward for a space, yet the 'merchant' knew we had come from the south."

"I remembered these things when I saw the pearls," Taikal said. "But who was this man who took such pains to follow and slay us? By now the river has carried his body far in the opposite direction, and we can not spend days looking for it."

"He kept his face hidden from us, both as 'scholar' and 'merchant,' " said Yarkut. "But that could have been because we would have recognized him as a Mongol, even if we did not know him. When he spoke to us tonight, we surely would have found his voice familiar if he had been someone we knew."

Taikal shook his head. "He spoke in Arabic. Would you recognize even a friend's voice if he used a different tongue?"

"No," Yarkut admitted. "The rhythm of his speech would be altered then. So this man could be someone we knew. Or," he added as a thought struck him, "perhaps we might have recognized him as someone's companion, for we know not if our follower was alone responsible for the strange happenings on the drive line."

"I think the man really responsible sent this one after us," Taikal said. "Remember, there was one panda yet living beyond the drive line. The man responsible would surely be anxious to remain with the hunt so he could care for the animal in some way. Perhaps he has even brought the panda back across the line and has hidden it in the same fashion as before."

"He could easily have invented some excuse to persuade our follower to slay us on the trail," Yarkut said. "The man who died tonight might indeed have been innocent of the whole affair."

"I had not thought of that," Taikal admitted. "Yet he must have realized all was not well if he accepted the task of fol-

lowing us. Anyone else would have gone to Genghis Khan
with a charge against us, and then soldiers would have been
sent. Indeed, if stealing and the thought of murder came so
easily to him, he would not turn from a scheme that used
viciously trained animals."

"If there is another man directing the pandas, I fear when
we return we may find there have been more deaths from
savage attacks," said Yarkut. "Perhaps our leaving was a
signal to him to finish his work before others became suspicious." He began scrubbing his *tsamba* bowl with sand.
"Once I told you, Taikal, that two attacks against two generals was only coincidence. Now I wonder if the person responsible is really working for the Karakhitaians. Three
pandas were sent to Gutchluk over a year ago; that would
give him enough time to contrive a plot."

"Perhaps," Taikal said thoughtfully. "Though surely it
would take more than gold to make a Mongol turn traitor."
Then he shook his head. "No, that is a clumsy way of killing
enemies."

"Gutchluk has had little success in battle. Even our losses
this summer brought him only a truce," Yarkut reminded
him. "But if our generals were killed, we would do so poorly
next summer that Gutchluk would at least win a permanent
truce from the Khan even if he did not defeat us. And,
Taikal, Gutchluk knows our customs in hunting."

"You think, then, that he uses trained animals as a weapon
against soldiers who may not kill?" Taikal stirred up the
fire. "The murderer in our camp surely could not accomplish
his purpose without help from Kara Khitai, though whether
he or Gutchluk thought of the idea first I do not know."

"That matters not," said Yarkut.

"But it does matter," Taikal insisted. "If the man went to Gutchluk with his plot, he must have had a deeper purpose than mere gold. Then if we can discover who has such a reason, our work is made simpler."

"I know of no one who would have such a reason," Yarkut said. "And questioning twenty-six thousand warriors is impossible."

"Then let us begin from the other end," suggested Taikal. "Who could have had contact with the Karakhitaians?"

"The number runs into hundreds," Yarkut said. "For almost all of Jiemdad's regiment was captured, as was the commander himself. Even Haroun was among them."

"The lute-singer was captured?"

"Did you not know? Haroun, like many minstrels, rode with the troops all summer. But he alone had the courage to watch each battle, for he stayed with the messengers posted nearby. When Jiemdad's regiment was captured, the rush of the Karakhitaians took them beyond the battlefield, and so they rounded up the messengers too."

"Was he among the men when Bayan came to their rescue?"

"Certainly," Yarkut replied. "Some of the captured soldiers mentioned that the Karakhitaians even let Haroun continue his singing, as he was an artisan and not a warrior."

"I think we may forget Haroun," Taikal said. "His successful traveling depends on his not becoming a party to intrigues. Besides, he told us of the beast in the Potala and even warned us of danger on the caravan trail, though he did not know of the Burkhan-Buddha."

"Lin-nam lived in Kara Khitai until the end of this summer, when he joined us," Yarkut said. "If he had been born in the Kin Empire in northern Cathay, I would say that he desired revenge for the Khan's having conquered that country not long ago. But Lin-nam was raised in the south, in the Sung Empire, though as a child he moved to Kara Khitai with his family. And he is an animal trainer."

"So is Basukor," Taikal said. "And he was with the army all summer."

"I do not think Basukor was taken by Karakhitaians at any time," said Yarkut. "He stayed with the herders and the supply wagons, which are always well hidden before a battle. Nor have I heard of the capture of any of these stores."

"That would not prevent any messages from being passed between him and Gutchluk," Taikal pointed out. "The man who followed us was a warrior, and Basukor could have used him to send word to Gutchluk of his willingness to play traitor."

"Basukor would have a reason for doing this," Yarkut admitted. "Since early manhood he has not been able to ride with the army. Perhaps he became jealous of the successful warriors and chose this means of exercising power." Then he shook his head. "But he has power enough now, if that is what he wanted, for many warriors hang upon his foolish words."

"The black dye!" Taikal exclaimed. "I had nearly forgotten that. It was Basukor who bought cheap dye from the Muscovite."

"It was used, of course, to disguise the panda while the animal was slipped through the picket line," said Yarkut. "But was Basukor the only one who bought such dye?"

"There were six or seven altogether," Taikal replied. "Some dye had been bought before the drive ever started. But about the time the pandas were seen, Basukor purchased some, as did Lin-nam. I did not listen to the other names, for I was convinced that Basukor was the one responsible."

"It does seem most likely that he caused the charges," Yarkut admitted. "Yet how could he have gotten the animals in his possession? Lin-nam, on the other hand, came directly from Kara Khitai with his cart."

"Could not the beasts have been kept in some cave just inside Kara Khitai's boundary?" suggested Taikal. "Then once the drive began, the animals could easily have been moved up every day or so, to be housed in a new cave discovered during the day's travel."

"Then anyone could be responsible for the beasts," Yarkut said. "Not only Basukor, but the other men who bought the Muscovite's dye. For that matter, a servant or a friend could have been sent to purchase the coloring."

Taikal nodded. "We must question the Muscovite again when we return. Let us go on, for dawn is but two hours away." He began rolling up his blankets.

"Taikal, what will we do with the pearls? I do not care to possess stolen wealth."

"Does not this trail take us through Angrisha La? The salt gatherer said his family lived there with its herds."

"They will be glad to see the pearls again. Perhaps we can also leave the tent and extra horses with them," said Yarkut.

Two days and nights of continual riding took them across rivers and plains, then up into the Bayan Kara Mountains. At Angrisha La the salt gatherer was overjoyed to recover his possessions. The cadets stayed overnight with the family, and the next day they were sent off with enough provisions to last them for the rest of their journey.

They rode north steadily, shifting slightly eastward to meet the drive on its approach to Karakorum.

And then one night they thundered over a last concealing hill. On the broad plain below winked thousands of fires.

"There is the camp," Yarkut shouted as they galloped down the hill.

"We have been gone three and a half weeks," Taikal said. "I wonder what has happened in our absence."

"So you return," said the lieutenant in charge of the supply carts when the cadets came to claim their belongings. "And is Gutchluk in good health? Or did you ride to Cathay?"

"Yes, we had a pleasant trip," said Yarkut, as if in answer to friendly questions. "But let us have our camping equipment, for we are tired."

"It is a long way to Urgendj," said Taikal in sudden inspiration.

The lieutenant looked up in surprise as he handed them their possessions. "So your mission took you to the Kharesm Shah! Will the Shah fight alongside us next year?"

"We know nothing of politics," Taikal said hastily, as if covering some slip of the tongue. "Will you not ask the Master of Provisions to send us a sheep haunch?"

"Gladly," the lieutenant replied, impressed by their supposed mission. He shook his head as Yarkut held out their sheepskins toward him. "Keep your winter clothing with you. The weather has become much colder, and Basukor predicts a bad snowstorm soon."

Taikal and Yarkut selected a place for their yurt and set it up. Their neighbors, sitting around their outside fires, glanced at them curiously and began lowering their voices. Yarkut leaned close to Taikal. "Word will soon pass that we have gone to treat with the Kharesm Shah," he whispered

153

with a grin. "This will conceal our real destination. That was a fine idea of yours!"

They had a fire going by the time a boy came with their food. Taikal cut some of the meat in thin slices so it would be finished while the rest was still roasting. "I hunger for fresh meat," he said, spearing the slices with sharpened sticks and setting them against the flames. "But do not think I was ungrateful for the salt gatherer's supplies, for not only did we save money but we made better time, since we did not have to stop to buy food."

Yarkut pulled wonderful things from the bundle the Master of Provisions had sent. "Two sacks of fresh milk! A bag of dried fruit. A package of nuts. A bunch of onions. Taikal, we will have a feast!"

They ate long and heartily until they groaned at the thought of more food. "Now for a real night's rest," said Yarkut happily.

"I have to send a report to the Khan," Taikal remembered. "It will not take long, for there is little to add to the Pandit Ch'en Po's letter."

"You can tell of the man who followed us," Yarkut said.

"What can I say but that we met someone who tried to kill us and that we found danger on the trail? These are events normal to long journeys. The Khan would not care to hear of our guesses. It would look as if we were seeking importance."

"Write what you will." Yarkut yawned. "But remember to mention the gift the Pandit Ch'en Po is sending to Genghis Khan. Post riders must be sent out so the Tibetans will receive help on the trail after they leave their country."

"There is still much to be done before we may sleep,"

Taikal said, rubbing his tired eyes. "We must relieve the men we put in our places on the drive line. And we want to question the Muscovite. We should seek out Haroun, too, and learn what has passed in our absence."

"Tomorrow, tomorrow," Yarkut said. He went into the yurt, handing out the writing materials to his friend.

Taikal scribbled a hasty report and sealed it. Calling a passing messenger, he gave him his report and the Pandit Ch'en Po's letter. He kicked dirt over the fire and went into the yurt, with hardly enough strength left to take off his boots.

Drums awakened Taikal and Yarkut early the next morning. For several moments they lay and listened to sounds of men rising and lighting their cooking fires. "I could sleep the whole day," said Yarkut.

Taikal stirred tiredly. "Be thankful we can ride slowly today. And we will have a short rest from trail food."

They boiled a great quantity of rice, putting half of it in sacks for the day's ride, along with chunks of cold mutton. Between them they finished the last of the fresh milk. "I wish we still had some of that tea," said Yarkut. "A hot drink would be a fine way to start the morning. It has indeed grown colder since we left."

By the time a herdboy had brought them horses and hunting weapons, their yurt was down, rolled into a neat bundle and placed with their blankets and other possessions that the supply carts would pick up. Quickly they saddled, tying on their food sacks and sheepskins. They separated to find the officers they had appointed in their places.

Taikal's horse carefully picked its way among fires and yurts, or ashes and bundles where they had been. Men milled around, walking out for horses, visiting friends, or still enjoying the morning meal. Seeing the man from his squad to whom he had delegated his command, Taikal trotted over and dismounted before his fire.

"I have returned to my command," Taikal said. "And I would like a report of what has happened in my absence."

The man glanced up with a hint of amusement in his eyes. "What has happened is that you no longer have a command," he said, cutting up some meat into his rice bowl.

"Do you mean that Jiemdad has put someone else in my place?" asked Taikal.

The man shook his head. "Our squad no longer exists. We soldiers have been used to replace others injured during the drive."

"That is not the custom," said Taikal. "Units are usually not reformed until the next summer's war."

The warrior shrugged. "You must see our commander about that." He bent over his rice bowl, eating rapidly.

Taikal trotted away, anger burning within him. Now he was without any command at all. Up to now during the hunt he had exercized authority only three weeks. The other cadets his age would soon be so far ahead of him in experience that he would never catch up. Perhaps that was Jiemdad's plan. Taikal knew now that the commander had never forgotten that the son of a common soldier had escorted him back from his captivity.

The camp was rapidly breaking up. Many of the soldiers were on horseback, beginning to assemble in their units. Taikal glanced at two or three white horsetail crests and finally found beneath one the face he sought.

He rode over to Jiemdad, saluting him respectfully. The commander let him wait while he issued orders to several captains. When they left, Jiemdad turned to Taikal. "So home is best after all," he said.

"The man I had put in charge of my squad during my absence says that the unit no longer exists," said Taikal.

"I had no way of knowing if you intended to return," Jiemdad replied. "You did not consult me when you left."

"There was no need, since the Khan knew of my plans," Taikal said. By the sudden flicker in Jiemdad's eyes Taikal knew he had heard the rumor of their being sent to Kharesmia. "I have come to ask what position I will hold on the drive line."

"I have nothing for you but the post of warrior," Jiemdad said, with just the hint of respect in his voice. "But we have had many injuries of late, for the animals know they are being driven. If some lieutenant breaks a leg, you might take his place." He pointed out a squad that had assembled nearby. "You may ride with that unit."

Taikal trotted over with misgivings, for the lieutenant of the squad wore the red crest of the cadet officers. He recognized Manuli, a cadet who had continued to jeer him in Karakorum long after the others had ceased.

"Jiemdad is indeed trying my skill if he sends you to me," said Manuli with heavy scorn. "I have spent over six weeks making this squad the best unit in the regiment. Take care you do not disgrace me, Taikal, or it will go hard with you."

Taikal went to take his place in the squad, but Manuli called him back. "You must take off your crest," commanded the youth. "Or you might be tempted to play my part during some emergency."

Taikal took off his helmet and removed his crest. "Emergency or no, Manuli, I would never care to be mistaken for you." He trotted to his place before the cadet lieutenant could master his anger for a suitable reply.

A captain rode up to speak to Manuli, and Taikal was relieved that it was not Pechen. Though Jiemdad had treated him with less contempt today, Taikal knew the commander was not above letting Pechen do his insulting.

Manuli bawled orders. The squad smartly wheeled horses and trotted to where its company was forming. Taikal saw that the other nine companies of Jiemdad's regiment were also assembling. The commander himself paced restlessly on his horse.

"Why are we in regimental formation?" Taikal asked the man next to him.

"Perhaps Jiemdad is going to make another announcement," the warrior answered. "There was one over a week ago, about Basukor."

The captain of Taikal's company faced his men and unrolled a sheet of parchment. The other captains were breaking the seals of similar scrolls.

" 'Men of my regiment, sturdy warriors!' " the captain began reading. "Have you so soon forgotten my words? I counseled you not ten days ago to remember you are the warriors of Genghis Khan, the most valiant soldiers who have ever been led to the battlefield.

" 'In battle you know not fear, and you face death joyously. Yet there is a man in our camp who does not draw the bowstring, nor does he hurl the lance, and this man has made many of you afraid. Basukor says he has power, and he tells you to fear him. He commands you to purchase protection from him.

" 'Basukor enslaves you with words and trickery. When you give him money you are but buying more fear. Remember that only living foes can bring you harm, and you have already proven that you can vanquish your enemies. Cast away your charms and idols! Heed not Basukor's false words, and go forth in valor.' "

Taikal listened with growing surprise. He had not known that Jiemdad was much concerned with events in the camp. Perhaps it was this new anxiety which had lessened his wish to revenge himself on Taikal.

Dismissed, the companies broke up to take their places in the drive line. Taikal noticed that some of the men quietly discarded felt idols and the "magic charms" Basukor made from hair, bone, feathers, and other trash in the camp. But other warriors, untying the amulets from their saddles, quickly thrust them inside their jackets.

As they waited for the signal that would start the day's drive, Taikal asked the man next to him, "What has turned Jiemdad against Basukor?"

"Nothing," the warrior replied. "But Jiemdad has never liked this growing concern over the magician's spirits. He says it weakens fighting men, and perhaps he is right. We have had more accidents of late, for men are either over-confident from carrying charms or timid because they do not."

Messengers went up and down the line with their reports. The herds and wagons were already moving out.

"What is the position of the line?" Taikal asked his companion.

"The circle is not yet fully formed," the man replied. "There is a gap of some miles, and we must draw closer to Karakorum before it is closed. Next week men will begin dropping out as the ring is made and drawn tighter."

Suddenly drums rattled and cymbals crashed. The drive

line moved forward. Taikal braced his padded lance under his arm, already falling into the familiar rhythm of the hunt. At first Manuli rode near him, criticizing and continually shouting orders. But when a fox nearly slipped through the other end of the squad, the cadet lieutenant began to pay more attention to the rest of his men.

The hunt was noisier than when Taikal and Yarkut had left the drive. The animals snarled, howled, or grunted as they ran. More of them faced the line and charged. Cymbals crashed incessantly to turn them back or stir up the ones which gave up and lay down before the horses.

The necessary alertness was a strain for Taikal after his rugged journey to the Roof of the World. By the end of the day, after helping picket the extra mounts in line, he was completely exhausted. When the camping order was given, Taikal slipped away quickly before Manuli could put him on sentry duty.

Wearily he claimed his and Yarkut's possessions and set up the yurt. He had the meat roasting by the time his friend joined him.

"My company is on the farther end of the curving line," Yarkut said. "It was a long ride back here. Some of the men are putting up their yurts back there to save time." He glanced at Taikal's helmet. "Taikal, where is your crest?"

Taikal told him how he lost his command and rode now as an ordinary soldier.

"That is too bad," Yarkut said. "And I am afraid my news is no more cheerful than ours. The Muscovite furrier who sold the cheap black dye is gone."

"I knew we should have seen him last night!"

"He left shortly after we went off on our journey," Yarkut

replied. "Before Jiemdad began speaking to our regiment, I went looking for the Muscovite. A gem cutter who used to share meals with him told me that the furrier became anxious because so many people had bought his cheap dye. Fearing he would soon be accused of cheating—for he did not know if his Arabic were good enough to explain—he fled down the trail to Samarkand three weeks ago."

"Someone must have threatened him," Taikal said. "Perhaps I was seen talking to the man." He stared at his meal without interest. "Every time we have proof that someone is responsible for the black and white beast, the proof is snatched from us."

A chord rippled from a lute. They looked up to find Haroun. "May I beg a meal for a song?" he asked.

They filled an extra bowl with meat and rice. "You are welcome, song or no, Haroun," Yarkut said, handing him a horn of rice wine.

"Men say you were sent to see the Kharesm Shah," the singer told them. "Some take this as a sign that Genghis Khan has forgiven Taikal's killing the mysterious beast. Has your journey gone well?"

"Well enough as journeys go," Yarkut replied cautiously.

"Your song proved true, Haroun," Taikal said. "But more we can not say."

He nodded understandingly. "It was a pity you had to miss Basukor's grand entertainment. He did summon Beishung and magically slew the beast. The skin—"

"Summoned *who?*" they cried together.

"Beishung," repeated Haroun. "That is what Basukor now calls the black and white beast. It is the principal idol in his magic. Now instead of fearing all his spirits, we need treat only with Beishung, the most powerful."

Taikal tried to keep his voice steady. "How did Basukor come by this word?"

"It is not a word; it is his name for this newly contrived spirit," Haroun explained.

"Have you never heard of this name in all your travels, Haroun?" Yarkut asked.

The lute-singer shook his head. "Does it mean something?"

Yarkut deftly avoided answering the question. "How did Basukor make the beast appear? Was there a third attack on the drive line?"

"There did happen to be some trouble on the picket line. Twice horses tore loose and went into the hunt area. Later on during the drive it was found that the black and white animal had slain and devoured the runaway horses. But this happened in the week you left the camp and has nothing to do with Basukor's trick.

"One night, when there was no moon, Basukor summoned a great crowd. He used many colored powders in his fire pots, and his servants clashed their cymbals and banged their drums with commendable energy."

"Servants?" asked Taikal. "Then he has more than one?"

"There is the Uigurian boy, an aged Karait woman who does the cooking and sewing, and a Tangut herder who cares for Basukor's sheep and horses. These three live in the yurt Basukor used to use for his divination, for now he has a much grander one. Yes, our magician friend has grown wealthy in a short time.

"On this night the old woman and the boy were banging away while the Tangut fingered a weird tune on his flute. Basukor limped about the platform of his new yurt cart, muttering spells and flinging incense into the braziers. Colored smoke soon made a tent over the crowd, and the smell of incense became heavy indeed. The magician was dressed in a robe of feathers to which were sewn some bits of shining material, so that when he whirled in his awkward prance I soon became dizzy with the sparkle.

"He had the crowd learn a chant, shouting the phrases to them. Soon everyone was clapping hands and yelling out these nonsense words. Many began to swoon, either from excitement or the suffocating incense. By now there was so much smoke and noise that I could not keep as careful a watch on Basukor's actions as I had hoped.

"Suddenly the magician flung apart his hands and bellowed at the top of his lungs, 'Beishung! Beishung!' The crowd took up the cry, though no one seemed to know what the word meant. Then a gong sounded, and at once everyone fell silent. In the space before Basukor's yurt, which had been kept clear by burning fires around it, I saw a black and white beast such as you slew, Taikal."

"Was it alive?"

"It seemed to be, for it moved just as a real, living animal would," Haroun said. "I thought I even heard it growl."

"Where were Basukor and his three servants when the beast appeared?" Yarkut asked.

"I know not for certain," replied the lute-singer. "While I was struggling forward to gain a better view, those nearest the beast fell back against their neighbors. Besides, it is difficult to keep one's wits clear during such confusion as I witnessed that night.

"But I do remember Basukor crying out, 'Beishung, give yourself to me!' I heard the clap of hands, and suddenly the creature fell as if stricken dead. Then for an instant I saw Basukor at the edge of his platform. He flung out his hands, and colored smoke issued from the fires around the space where the beast had fallen. When the vapor cleared, the beast had disappeared. Basukor had gone inside his yurt. The Uigurian lad announced that his master was ready to sell charms, and then all three servants once more applied themselves to their instruments. I left as soon as I could get free of the crowd."

"How did the people know that the black and white creature was really the same as that which charged the drive line?" asked Taikal. "Could not Basukor have disguised some other animal to play the part?"

"I do not think anyone questioned it," Haroun replied. "Besides, the next day Basukor hung up on his yurt the skin of his Beishung. I myself examined it. Indeed, the pelt was genuine, even to the cut where Basukor said the invisible Sword of Heaven pierced the animal."

"Does the skin still hang there for all to see?" asked Yarkut.

Haroun shook his head. "Only for one day was it shown. But he has twice worn the skin as a cloak when making announcements."

"Did he predict a snowstorm?" asked Yarkut with a grin.

The lute-singer nodded. "Though it is cold enough for snow without a magician's help. The other announcement was that great danger would lurk in the hunt ring."

"Of course there will be danger in the hunt ring!" Taikal laughed. "But how can Basukor make people believe he really causes things that would happen without him?"

"I have seen people believe things even more foolish than that, Taikal. We three, and many other stronger men, know that Basukor's 'displays of power' would happen anyway, and we realize his Beishung was the result of clever shamming. But people anxious to believe that they can harm enemies or change their luck with spells will also believe the other things Basukor tells them. They are really using this magic nonsense to excuse their own faults and weaknesses. Instead of trying to live up to the high codes of conduct taught by religious men, they find it easier to turn to superstition. If brought to their senses, they would see at once that they were only letting someone take advantage of them."

"What fee does Basukor charge for his consultations?" Taikal asked.

The lute-singer told him. "But that is only for simple incantations to change luck or to find lost articles. According to what I have heard, the fee is higher if a man has a spell woven against an enemy or a charm made to ward off a spell which was woven against him." Haroun grinned. "And then, I doubt not, the enemy comes back for an incantation which will make the protective charm worthless against the original spell."

"No wonder Basukor has become wealthy in such a short time," Yarkut said.

Someone shouted a summons to Haroun. The singer rose and left, sweeping chords from his lute as he joined several men seated around a fire.

"How did Basukor learn the word beishung?" Yarkut asked. "I have not heard that he traveled into Tibet or to the Sung Empire."

"Gutchluk could have told him," Taikal answered. "The adventurer who brought him the pandas must have called them beishungs."

"I am surprised that Haroun did not recognize the name," Yarkut said. "Surely the lama who told him of the beast in the Potala also told him the other names the beast bears."

Taikal shrugged. "Haroun did not even know it was called a panda. He is interested only in songs. But Lin-nam came from the Sung Empire."

"He moved to Kara Khitai when he was a child. Of course, his father could have told him tales of his native land, including the 'mythical' beishung of the forest. For that matter, Basukor could have met some traveler years before who told him such a tale. We can not use this name as proof that Basukor or someone else is working with the Karakhitaians."

"No, but the skin might be proof," Taikal replied. "If it is a real beishung skin, it must bear marks of its captivity. We must visit Basukor, and while one of us does business with him, the other will find and examine the pelt."

"What reason can we give Basukor for consulting him?"

Taikal grinned. "I slew Beishung, did I not? Since then my luck has been bad. I lost my company, and now I have lost my squad. I must purchase a change of fortune."

Counting their money, they found they could meet the spirit-talker's price. "But it is well," said Yarkut, "that the Paymaster comes around tomorrow."

Seeking out Basukor's yurt, they found that Haroun was right. The magician's new residence was as large as a household yurt. It was mounted on a great wagon covered to the ground with black cloth. The felt dome was magnificently painted in gold, with strange designs of red and silver. His old yurt, occupied now by the servants, was drawn up nearby.

Warriors stood around Basukor's yurt, each waiting his turn. Whenever a man entered, the Uigurian boy on the platform of the cart struck a small gong.

When Taikal and Yarkut entered the yurt, it was entirely

dark. Taikal heard the entrance flap drop into place behind them. Then, with startling suddenness, six braziers burst into flame, revealing Basukor sitting on a stool shrouded with expensive tapestry. Wrapped in fine Cathayan silks, with a carved likeness of the beishung head for a hat, the magician intoned, "Advance into the realm of Beishung."

They walked toward him. Like all family dwellings, the yurt was partitioned with hangings on three sides. Normally these compartments were the sleeping quarters of the family, but Basukor probably used the rooms to store the ingredients of his trickery. These curtains were of silk, and they billowed and sagged gently, though there was no draft.

Taikal felt a stab of resentment when he and Yarkut reached an embroidered cushion set before Basukor. Was he to kneel to this charlatan? Yet he had come to play a part. He fell to his knees, bowing deeply. Yarkut knelt to one side, on the carpeted floor of the wagon.

"You have come," the spirit-talker said in measured tones, "to beg forgiveness for having slain Beishung's mortal carcass. You come in fear, Taikal, for you have brought a friend to sustain you in your trial."

Taikal suppressed a smile. Basukor was an actor worthy of the Cathayan stage! He fumbled for his moneybag. "I bring but a pittance, for it is all I have."

"That matters not." Basukor deftly swept the bag into his hand, swiftly computed the amount by its weight, and made it disappear into his garments. "You come with a contrite heart, and if you but follow instructions, Beishung will look upon you with favor. Bad luck has followed you as a wolf follows a stray sheep. You have lost your cadet command. Your long journey was filled with danger. But now this ill-fortune will change."

From a small chest near his stool, the magician withdrew bowls containing mysterious ingredients. He kindled a small fire in a brazier before him. Muttering strange words, he cast into the flames what to Taikal seemed to be scraps of leather, feathers, shards of bone. All of these materials had been fashioned into shapes—squares, circles, crescent moons, and stars.

Basukor handed Taikal a rattle strangely decorated and gave a tiny string of bells to Yarkut. "Shake the rattle and the bells without pause, for by this means we are protected against the wrath of Beishung while I make the incantation." Casting a handful of incense into the brazier, he drew forth a small drum and began tapping out an intricate pattern of sound. "Begin now," he commanded the cadets.

With rattle and bells, Taikal and Yarkut soon fell into the rhythm of the magician's drumming. The sweet odor of incense began coiling through the yurt.

The charlatan began chanting unknown syllables, his voice rising and falling. From time to time he threw into the brass bowl more powders and incense. Soon a pall of smoke hung between Basukor and his visitors.

Slowly Taikal stretched out his hand and took the bells from Yarkut, copying the rhythm his friend used. He watched as Yarkut carefully edged toward the curtain at the side of the yurt. Basukor's incantation had reached an intense pitch. Dimly through the smoke Taikal saw him swaying in time to his drumming. Taikal nodded to Yarkut. His friend slipped beneath the silken curtain.

Taikal concentrated on shaking the bells and rattle, for he realized that any fault of the rhythm would warn Basukor that someone had moved out of place. The moments wore hard on his nerves, for he feared that at any moment the magician would cease chanting.

The curtain where Yarkut had entered the adjoining compartment began bulging a little faster and more unevenly than it had before. Once when it dropped back into place, Taikal clearly saw the crouching form of his friend.

Basukor began calling out the name of his spirit. "Beishung! Beishung!"

Then for one startled moment Taikal nearly dropped the rattle and bells. Yarkut had accidentally pushed the head of the beishung pelt out into plain sight.

At that moment three knocks were sounded on the floor of the cart.

Basukor sprang up through the pall of smoke, his expression of mystic concentration replaced with a look of fury. "Where is the other one?" he shouted, reaching out for Taikal. "What are you trying to do?"

Taikal twisted away from Basukor's clutching hands. The magician moved forward, anger distorting his features. "Where has he gone?" Basukor demanded.

"My friend was frightened away," Taikal said. Then simulating horror, he pointed to the beishung pelt lying beyond the curtain. "But look!" he cried. "Beishung comes! Away, away! Save yourself!"

Turning, he ran out of the yurt, flinging aside the entrance flap. He jumped off the platform and quickly lost himself in a troupe of strolling entertainers.

He waited a long time at the trail yurt until Yarkut finally joined him. They went inside so they would not be seen and perhaps overheard by one of Basukor's servants.

"The pelt is a real one, Taikal. And it does bear marks of captivity. I could see where the creature had once worn a collar and several places where it had been jabbed with a goad. There was also a sword slash, just as Haroun had told us. I was almost tempted to take the skin with me so that for once our proof would be safe."

"Basukor will guard it well for his own reasons," said Taikal. "And he will have to produce it if the Khan so commands. But how was it that the head slipped from beneath the curtain?"

"The yurt is curtained with the usual thick felt," Yarkut explained. "Those silken hangings were then placed outside the real partitions. By the way, there are cords sewn to the silk at various points, and when they are pulled, the hangings move as if by spirits' hands. I followed some of the cords to a hole in the floor of the cart. No doubt Basukor's old woman sits beneath the wagon and works the cords.

"I easily found the beishung pelt behind the felt curtain, for Basukor keeps it close at hand. To get the light I needed, I moved between the silk curtain and the felt. There I could make out the scars.

"Meanwhile I kept getting tangled in those moving cords. I must have pulled on them in freeing myself, for suddenly the person underneath the wagon knocked a warning to Basukor.

"When I heard you shout, I saw that I had let the pelt slip out from behind the curtain. I at once went under the felt partition and then out beneath the yurt wall. I jumped off the cart and walked away quickly before Basukor or his servants could catch sight of me."

"Since the pelt Basukor possesses is real, then all the animals are accounted for," said Taikal. "Three beishungs were sent to Kara Khitai. I slew one; the other is still before the drive line, and Basukor sacrificed the third for his trick."

"Unless Basukor brought the second beast back through the picket line for his trick," Yarkut suggested. "Haroun told us that the beast killed two horses some time ago, but there have been no recent disturbances. Either the animal has starved by now, or Basukor slew it for his illusion."

"Perhaps," Taikal admitted. "But might not the beishung find food among the animals which the drive line is encircling day by day?"

"Then why should it attack two horses from the picket line?" Yarkut countered. "It seems to me that someone released those horses, perhaps using the musk to make the prey

attractive. It might be that the sentries commented on the
scent, or Basukor feared they would soon notice it and remember the same odor near Chepe Noyon and Bayan when
they were attacked. Rather than let the beishung starve, he
used it to increase his prestige."

"We could be certain of your idea if we found some sentries who would recognize the musk scent I brought from
Tibet," said Taikal. "Yet I fear this would make our plans
known, and our hope of catching Basukor lies in surprising
him." Taikal stared at the flickering sheep-fat lamp which
lighted their yurt. "If you are right, Yarkut, the third animal
is being kept behind the drive line. If only we could find it!"

"That would mean searching every cave and thicket in
these hills," Yarkut said. "We will have to wait until some
incident leads us to the beast."

The next afternoon a sudden snowstorm struck the hunters. While the icy wind howled, the riders put on their
sheepskins and rode on. The cry for mattocks was heard
more frequently that day as animals burrowed into various
shelters. When the storm ended that evening, the moon came
out bright and clear. Yarkut and Taikal saddled horses and
rode out on the snowy slopes behind the sprawling camp,
but they could find no track resembling that of a beishung.

"Then my idea was wrong," said Yarkut. "The beast ahead
of the drive line still lives."

"The more I think of your suggestion, the more I am convinced that you are right," Taikal said. "But this means that
the animal is not hidden in caves along the way. Basukor
could not leave the moving of the creature for tomorrow,
for then there will be too much distance to cover in one
night."

"He could send his herder for it tomorrow morning,"
Yarkut pointed out. "If the Tangut kept to the woods, he
could bring the beishung quite close without being seen
during the day."

The morning brought a warm sun which quickly melted
the snow. Grassy slopes were slippery from the water, and
in many places mud was churned by the men and horses in
the camp. As Taikal rode toward the drive line, he saw
Chepe Noyon conferring with his commanders. The general no longer wore a sling, though he braced his left arm on
his broad leather belt.

Just before the drive began, Yarkut trotted up to where
Taikal sat his horse in Manuli's squad. "Chepe Noyon's
orders are to drive on as usual, for the Khan is anxious to
close the circle." In a lower voice he continued, "The Tangut has gone ahead with the carts. It will be difficult for him
to leave without arousing suspicion."

"Perhaps the old woman has been sent," Taikal suggested.

"She is driving one of Basukor's yurts, and the boy handles
the other," Yarkut replied.

The day's hunting became a disagreeable chore. The
horses slipped continually on the slick grass and in the mud.
Two of the mounts in Taikal's company were seriously injured and had to be slain.

When evening came, the hunters had not yet reached the
chosen camping area and had to drive on with flickering
torches and weary horses.

At last the yurts were set up along the sharply curving
drive line. There was little visiting and merriment in the
camp, the men preferring to sit quietly by the fire with their
late meal or passively watch some entertainment. Basukor

drove his magnificent yurt through the camp, calling his ability, but this night most of the soldiers were too weary for fear or hope.

Taikal and Yarkut joined the small crowd watching Lin-nam put his bears through their dances and tricks.

"I thought Lin-nam had three dancing bears," Taikal said.

"He sold one some time ago," Yarkut replied. "That reminds me. He does not know the word 'beishung.' I asked him that night we visited Basukor. When I left the magician's yurt I walked around looking for you, and I happened to come upon Lin-nam cleaning one of his cages. That is when he also told me he had sold the bears."

"There was more than one?"

"He sold one of the dancing bears and two fighting bears that he had in the second cage, the one that is always covered to keep the animals from becoming excited."

"Then how does he keep them from getting excited when he cleans their cage?"

"He has only one fighting bear left," Yarkut replied, tossing a coin into the arena after a particularly good trick by one of the bears. "This animal is taken out every second or third night to some secret place for additional training."

"Two gone, and one left," Taikal muttered. "Yarkut—"

"You do not think . . . ?" Yarkut's eyes widened.

"I will soon find out," Taikal replied, feeling in his clothing for the ivory vial he always kept there. He rose casually. "I will see you at our yurt."

He pushed his way through the watching crowd and walked across the narrow campsite. Gone was the great cluster of yurts and warriors, for by now the burning fires made a thin curving line, copying the nearly completed circle of picket horses which contained the driven game animals.

From the shadows of the carts ahead a man came toward him. Taikal saw that it was Haroun and greeted him. "Do the songs come hard tonight, Haroun?"

The singer struck a chord on his lute. "No, indeed, for I have sung yurts up and sung wood into fire. I have sung food down men's throats, the boots off their feet, and have even sung them to sleep. And I will sing the moon down if I can but keep my legs moving." He gestured beyond the shadowed wagons and made a gloomy face. "I left my mount behind, and the guards would not let me borrow an army horse, so I must walk the miles back to my own tent."

"The journey will be cheerful," Taikal said with a grin, "for you have a singer to lighten the way."

Haroun started out on his long walk, and Taikal sought out Lin-nam's bear wagons. Moonlight gleamed through the bars of an empty cage, though the other was still shrouded by its felt curtains. Taikal could hear nothing stirring within. Stooping, he pulled up a clump of grass by its roots.

Hearing a voice and the panting of dogs, Taikal quickly stepped into deep shadows. Not far away a Kashgai appeared with his trained dogs. The man put them in their cage, then fed and watered them. Petting and praising them for the night's work, the Kashgai let down the felt curtains, jumped out of the wagon, and put up the back end. He left, happily jingling his purse.

Taikal brought out the ivory vial, and unstoppering it, he spilled a little of the musk scent over the clod in his hand. A final glance around showed that he was completely alone. From beyond the wagons he could hear occasional sounds from the grazing droves, but there did not seem to be a herder nearby.

Taikal went up to Lin-nam's second cage and slipped the lump of scented earth between the bars, thrusting it under the edge of the felt cover.

A low rumble sounded behind the felt. Something began to stir behind the stout iron bars. Then there was the raking of claws on the floor of the cage. Suddenly the growling grew louder. The hidden animal threw itself against the bars, and the cage shuddered. In the moonlight Taikal could see the felt curtain press against the bars, then slacken as the beast drew back for another charge.

Taikal slipped away, keeping to the shadows of the wagons and carts. Behind, the animal's voice rose into a maddened roar. Beishung, niyalya-ponga, or panda—by whatever name it was called, Taikal had found the third arrow in Gutchluk's quiver.

Taikal stood at the edge of the camp to see if there were anyone about who might connect him with the disturbance. He could hear a crowd laugh at some joke in the shadow play. Fifes and drums spurred the dancing feet of the less weary warriors. But he could hear, too, the roaring of the beishung growing ever louder. Distantly dogs began barking.

As Taikal started back toward his yurt, a horseman came up and hailed him. It was Jiemdad.

"I have been seeking you, Taikal," said the commander. "Will you not be my guest tonight? There are some things I must discuss with you, but I will not keep you late."

"When shall I come to your yurt?" Taikal asked, torn between the need for showing courtesy to his commander and his desire to hasten far away from Lin-nam's carts. The beishung's roaring was now very noticeable, for some men were staring back at the line of wagons.

"Come now," urged Jiemdad. "But you will need a horse. Let us find a way through these wagons."

The commander paced his horse along the line of wagons, and Taikal followed reluctantly, for their direction took him back the way he had come. The roaring and the dogs' barking could not be ignored, and even the shuddering of the cage under the beast's charges could be heard. Jiemdad stopped his horse. "Here is a way through. Find a herder and have him bring you a horse. I will ride ahead and see what that disturbance is."

As Taikal started in search of a herder he could see men running toward Lin-nam's wagons. The Cathayan was foremost among them.

"Who is it?" demanded a voice from the shadows near Taikal. "Take care you do not frighten the herds!"

Startled, Taikal moved out into the moonlight. The other man did the same, and Taikal saw that he was Basukor's Tangut herder.

"Bring me an army horse," Taikal told him. "And a saddle for it, as I have left my own behind."

The Tangut peered suspiciously. "You are too young to be a soldier."

"I am a cadet."

"Your helmet lacks a crest."

"But helmet I have, and a sword to go with it. Fetch the horse," Taikal said in exasperation. He raised his voice after the grumbling herder. "And hurry!"

It seemed to take forever, and Taikal grew more ill at ease as torches lighted up the men clustering around Lin-nam's wagons. The peak of the beast's rage had passed, though it still growled and shook its cage. The excited dogs kept barking.

At last he saw the Tangut's shadow slowly moving toward him, leading a saddled horse. Taikal went up and took the reins from him.

"What is that commotion over there?" the herder asked as Taikal started off, leading the horse.

"Some trouble with the animals," Taikal called back. He blundered into the carts and went along them to find another opening. As he came between the wagons he saw that he was close to the crowd surrounding Lin-nam's cages. The felt still curtained the second cage. The Cathayan was urging everyone to leave, for their own noise would only further excite the fighting bear he had within.

The crowd began to thin out. Two men passed close to Taikal. "What did Lin-nam do with his dancing bears?" one asked the other.

"A lute-singer took charge of them so the Cathayan could run to his wagon. The singer has had some experience with bears."

The barking of the dogs began to die down. The Kashgai had run up to soothe them. The beishung had stopped charging the bars, though it still growled and occasionally raked the floor with its claws.

Taikal looked around for Jiemdad. Instead he saw Lin-nam walking toward him. "Is all well with your beast?" Taikal asked. He could not bring himself to call it a bear, now that he knew.

"Yes, it will soon fall asleep," the Cathayan replied. "You

were in this area, were you not, young master, when the bear became excited?"

"I went to the herds for a horse," he said in answer.

"Did you see anyone who might perhaps have teased the bear?" Lin-nam asked.

Taikal gestured out toward the herds. "I saw no one there but a herder, and he asked what the disturbance was."

"Then perhaps someone was hurrying past and bumped the wagon without meaning harm," Lin-nam suggested. "But I must be careful, for that fighting bear is of great value."

"I am certain this will not happen again," Taikal said with conviction. He swung into the saddle and bade the Cathayan good night.

Taikal found Jiemdad waiting where he had sent Taikal through the wagons for a horse. "I should have guessed that excitement of any kind draws youths," he said.

"I thought you might still be at the wagon," Taikal said as they rode through the camp.

Jiemdad flicked his reins in dismissal. "It was only some caged animal raising a howl. Its trainer soon came to quiet it."

Reaching the picket line, they followed it a long way, passing fires and yurts, and even Basukor's splendid dwelling. The Tangut herder was just dismounting before it.

Jiemdad commented on the progress of the hunt and the festival soon to come. Taikal answered agreeably, though he longed to be with Yarkut so they might discuss this latest discovery.

Jiemdad's field yurt was pitched fairly close to the picket line. Near it was the yurt of his personal attendants, the space between the two shelters having been turned into a small paddock where three or four horses were kept for convenience. A man ran up to take their horses, and they entered the yurt.

The cooking fire had died to a mass of glowing coals, but the field yurt was brightly lighted by a huge brass bowl in which burned the highly prized scented woods. The commander gestured Taikal toward an embroidered cushion and took his own place opposite. "It is time we came to an understanding," he said. "First let us drink to friendship." He clapped his hands, and a servant came from behind the single silken hanging which formed the sleeping compartment. Jiemdad gave orders, and soon Taikal found himself holding an ornamented horn filled to the brim with deep dark fluid.

"Drink," Jiemdad urged, lifting his own horn. "This is better than our rice wine, for it is pressed from the grapes that grow on the slopes of the Tien Shan. It is a rich wine."

It was stronger than rice wine too. Taikal gasped as he carelessly swallowed several gulps at once. "It is too strong for me," he said. "May I not have rice wine instead?"

"Rice wine is little better than water," Jiemdad replied with a trace of contempt. "But then I forget your youth."

The remark stung Taikal, and silently he held his horn out to be filled by the wine-bearer.

"Now we must have something to sharpen our taste." Jiemdad gestured, and his servant brought forth silver platters piled high with good things to eat.

Taikal could hardly choose among the rice and barley cakes, Cathayan candies, and the sweet almond paste of Samarkand. He found as he ate that the food helped take away the bite of the strong wine, and so he did not check the servant from again filling his horn. Jiemdad added more spices to the brazier, and soon Taikal found himself in a mellow mood.

"You must forgive me for having been so short-tempered with you," Jiemdad began. "But you must guess my feelings when the Karakhitaians at last released me. It was not pleasant for me, the Khan's own commander, to have taken their orders for several weeks."

"Perhaps I should have been less insistent on leading the escort," Taikal replied.

"I understand how a youth feels about his first command," Jiemdad replied. "Though I must confess it took me some time to overcome my own feelings in the matter. Yet you bore up well under the hard work I gave you after the Khan transferred you to my regiment."

This seemed to call for a return compliment. "It was generous of you to offer me leadership when the Khan would have withheld it entirely."

The commander waved aside Taikal's words. "My thoughts were not generous to begin with, but I soon saw you were a cadet of some merit. I was really sorry there was no place for you when you returned from your journey, but you will have a command tomorrow."

"A command?" The unexpected words whirled in his head.

"Yes, you will lead a company." Jiemdad suddenly smiled. "Do you think you can manage that?"

A company! Ten lieutenants beneath him! Taikal withheld the glad shout that welled within him and replied in the tones of a hardened warrior, "I will command them well. Was the other captain injured in the drive?"

Jiemdad shook his head. "His sister's husband died suddenly, and he asked if he might go to help her. This was some time ago, and only now have I received a message from him that he must remain with her longer than he had expected. His brother-in-law had many debts, and so his herds will have to be sold and other arrangements made. Until now I had one of his lieutenants acting as captain. But there is no longer reason not to give you a command." Jiemdad told him the location of his company. "Early tomorrow I will send word to the acting captain that you are to be in charge."

"I will not fail your confidence in me," Taikal promised. This very night he would fasten the red crest to his helmet.

"But enough of serious matters," Jiemdad said. "Let us celebrate your new leadership." He signaled his servant to fill both their horns, and they toasted each other warmly.

Jiemdad leaned forward confidentially. "Perhaps you think my change of heart is too sudden."

"No, no," Taikal said, but now that it had been suggested, he began to wonder.

"I feel certain I would have known your worth in time," the commander went on. "But the truth is that I was impressed that the Khan would entrust you with an important mission. It is said that you went to the country of the Kharesm Shah. Indeed, I have even heard stories of your pleasant stay in his palace at Urgendj."

So that was it! Taikal wanted to shout with laughter. An idle comment to a curious lieutenant had grown into a secret alliance with Shah Ala-u-Din. But it was an example of the power of rumor. No wonder Basukor's influence had grown!

Taikal made his face solemn. "It is not wise to believe everything that is said."

"True," Jiemdad agreed. "Nor would I have you betray any confidence. Yet the journey itself is remarkable for two cadets, skirting enemy country as you had to. Were you not pursued, or even followed, along the way?"

Another servant entered and went to Jiemdad's side.

"What is it?" the commander demanded, impatient at the interruption. The servant spoke into his ear, and Jiemdad nodded. "Forgive me for leaving," the commander said to Taikal. "I will be back shortly. Meanwhile, ask freely for wine and food." He rose and left the yurt, his servant following.

Taikal saw a pair of wooden gaming cubes where they had rolled under the silver brazier, and he idled away the time by trying to cast the same combination twice in a row. Occasionally the wine-bearer silently stepped forth and added more to Taikal's horn, and this made the cadet feel he must drink, although the warm glow had faded and he no longer cared for the wine.

At last Jiemdad returned. He signaled to the servant to pass the tray of sweets to his guest. "You must tell me of your journey," said the commander. "It is to be hoped that your cadet training helped you overcome the dangers on the way."

Taikal was suddenly weary of the pretense that circumstance had forced upon him. Yet this unearned prestige had brought him Jiemdad's friendship and a new command. He shrugged elaborately, and the sudden movement made him a little dizzy. "If there were danger, I took little notice, for my errand was foremost in my mind."

Jiemdad chuckled. "You are modest for such a young warrior. What, do you not wish to hear your name sung around campfires?"

"A loose tongue flies over the country like a falcon," Taikal said. Then fearing that his tone betrayed his resentment at Jiemdad's prying, he added, "When the time comes for words, I could not do better than tell my commander first."

"Well spoken!" Jiemdad said with a quick smile. "A commander's best officers are those who confide in him." He studied the gold band around his drinking horn. "You missed the fighting this summer. But surely next year you will need someone with whom to ride into battle."

"I ride with Chepe Noyon," Taikal replied.

"Of course. And how is our honored general? I have not seen much of him lately."

In spite of the heat and closeness in Jiemdad's yurt, Taikal could feel his face flaming. Since his return from Tibet he had seen the general only twice, and each time Chepe's haughty gaze showed that he had not yet forgotten his humiliation, even though he had lived to suffer it.

"Much will depend on how you manage your new company," Jiemdad said, covering Taikal's embarrassment. "And now you must know my custom in welcoming new officers to my regiment." He clapped his hands, and a servant glided into the yurt, his arms filled with articles.

"Gifts for the captain!" Jiemdad declared. "See the fine gold belt, the new sword. Here is a cloak of embroidered silk for festivals."

Dazed, Taikal touched the finery. "But, Jiemdad. . . ."

"Take them, they are yours!" Jiemdad laughed. "But you must repay me with your loyalty as long as you are under my orders. Now let us drink to success in the hunt."

Jiemdad pressed more wine upon Taikal and heaped fuel on the fire. He began boasting of his past battles and hunting drives. Once he referred to Basukor, and his face grew hard. Then he discussed the qualities of his horses. "My roan stallion—there is a horse! He is my favorite, and I will ride him into the hunt ring."

Taikal tried to enter the conversation, but his head whirled from the strong wine and the unaccustomed incense, so he merely nodded politely from time to time.

At last Jiemdad exclaimed, "The hour is late, Taikal. But you must come again soon."

Resisting an impulse to yawn, Taikal let Jiemdad guide him to the doorway of the yurt. His mount was led forth and the gifts tied securely to the saddle. Jiemdad shouted a hearty farewell as Taikal trotted off.

The cold air felt good, though Taikal could still smell the burning spices and feel the heat of the yurt fire. Jiemdad must have kept him later than he had intended, for nearly all the campfires were out. Taikal heard the distant hoofs of late-departing visitors, and somewhere wagon wheels creaked. The moon lighted the path behind the picket line as he put his horse into a canter.

Suddenly the night was disturbed by shouting. "The line, the line! Hold it!"

Horses screamed down the picket line, some plunging and pulling free of their tethers to scramble aside. Taikal came up to the scene, slowing his mount to a trot. Helmets gleamed in the moonlight as sentries came running. The picket horses beat their hoofs in frenzy.

There was a moving white patch, and Taikal heard a familiar snuffling. Then the white patch lunged clear of the shadows while its roars echoed through the night.

The black and white beast hurled itself at Taikal.

For a moment Taikal's scattered wits would allow him only to watch as the beishung quickly halved the space between them.

Then his horse reared, tearing the reins from his grasp.

Clear and horrible in his mind's eye, Taikal could see iron-hard claws raking Chepe Noyon's arm as the beast leaped for the general.

The beishung was almost upon him when Taikal kicked free of his stirrups and tumbled to the ground, rolling and rolling away from the terrible claws.

His horse screamed, its hoofs tearing the earth. The beast must be upon it now. The sentries' shouts grew louder, and when Taikal pushed himself to his feet he saw a knot of shield-bearers clustered around his mount. Torches moved through the night as soldiers ran up with padded lances.

The group of warriors struggled and jostled for position. The beast howled its rage above the whinny of horses. There was a scream, and the tight knot of men parted to let one of the soldiers stumble through, cradling a bloody arm.

Other warriors ran up to seize the hysterical picket horses. One of the torch-bearers worked his way through the group struggling with the beishung, holding high his flaming brand. Then there was triumphant shouting. The men surged forward. Taikal saw something white flashing over the moonlit field beyond. Warriors pulled up the picket horses.

"Double the guard!" ordered the sentry captain. "Call out the relief men."

Taikal went up to him. "Is my horse. . . ?"

"Dead, I fear. You barely escaped with your own life." He glanced beyond the picket line, at the now empty field. "The torchlight frightened the animal off, or we would still be fighting with it. I will get you another mount."

Taikal went to his torn and bloody horse and began taking off the saddle. Two soldiers helped him. The fine cloak he had received from Jiemdad was in shreds. The scabbard of the gift sword was scraped to the raw leather, and the gold belt showed deep tooth marks.

"The girth is deeply scarred," said a soldier who helped him saddle the new mount. "You must have it replaced before tomorrow's ride."

Thanking him for his help, Taikal rode away slowly, trying to keep his trembling hands from jerking the reins. Behind him in the still night air he could hear the excited talk of the sentries and the snorts of nervous horses.

Following the curve of the picket line, Taikal saw a brightly lighted dwelling come into view. It was Basukor's gilded household yurt. Nearby was the smaller white one of his servants. From the open doorways of both dwellings firelight streamed, and torches were fixed to the driving platforms. One or two other brands moved about in the darkness.

As Taikal approached, he saw Basukor on the platform of his golden yurt. The spirit-talker wore simple garments, and Taikal was surprised at how powerless he seemed in everyday garb. The old woman came from behind the cart with a torch in her hands, followed by the Uigurian lad. Then suddenly someone ran out of the dark near Taikal and seized his reins. His horse started, tossing its head. "Who are you?" cried the voice of Basukor's Tangut herder.

"A Mongol does not answer such demands," Taikal retorted.

The man crowded close to the saddle, peering upward in the moonlight. "You are the youth I saw near Lin-nam's carts tonight."

"And you are the herder who grumbles at fetching a horse," Taikal returned. "Let go of my reins!"

"I wish to speak with your companion," the herder said. At Taikal's puzzled pause, he added, "Then you ride alone? Have you seen no one around here of late?"

"What, has your master frightened away a customer before he was paid?" Taikal laughed. "I have seen nothing but sentries and horses."

The herder dropped the reins. "My anxiety has made me forget courtesy, young master. Sleep well tonight." Then he vanished into the darkness.

As Taikal rode on, a horseman slipped away from the picket line and joined him. "Is there some trouble at the yurt of Basukor?" The rider was Kishlik, the lieutenant who had helped Taikal lead the escort to rescue Jiemdad, and who had still spoken friendly words even after the black and white beast had been slain on the drive line.

"Only some customer who ran off without paying," Taikal said. "The Tangut asked if I had not seen the man."

Kishlik had just heard a report of the black and white beast charging through the picket line. "If you rode from that direction, Taikal, you must have heard the commotion."

"Indeed, Kishlik, I was attacked by the animal!"

"I heard that one of our cadets barely escaped death," Kishlik said. "You are fortunate indeed!"

"More fortunate than that," Taikal said with a grin. He remembered how Kishlik had warned him long ago that Jiemdad would become his enemy. "I have just come from toasting friendship with Jiemdad." He told the lieutenant of his new command.

Kishlik congratulated him heartily. "Yet do not let this attention make you foolish with pride. Jiemdad, I feel, is in a forgiving mood toward you because he is more concerned over Basukor's influence disrupting the discipline in his regiment."

"Perhaps you are right," Taikal agreed, though he sensed that Kishlik was really thinking of Taikal's rumored journey to the Kharesm Shah.

The lieutenant checked his horse. "I must speak with the sentry here. Good night, Taikal."

Taikal rode on to his trail yurt, too tired to turn his horse into the herds and walk back. A fire burned before the yurt, and huddling next to it, asleep, was Haroun. Taking off Jiemdad's gifts, Taikal unsaddled his mount. The horse snorted, freed of its bit, and the lute-singer awoke.

"So you are back, Taikal," said Haroun, stretching his limbs. "I did not have to wait long after all. Are you going to send that horse back to the herds? I would like to borrow it for my long ride back."

"You may have it if you turn it into the army herds. But I can not spare you a saddle, for I must return it tomorrow morning."

"I can ride well without saddle or bit." Haroun's tired

face lighted with a smile. "My thanks to you, Taikal."

Taikal put a rope halter on the horse, tethering the animal to one of the yurt pegs. "You need not have waited at all. Yarkut would have gotten a horse for you."

"I did not wish to disturb his sleep." Haroun gestured at a cut of mutton and a sack of milk Yarkut had left near the fire. "I knew one of you was still up, for surely this food is not a gift to Basukor's spirits."

Taikal divided the meat and gave half to Haroun. "What happened that you have not yet reached your own tent?"

"I had not walked far when I met a group determined to make merry until the sun rose. By the time I sang their flasks empty and their fire into embers, I was too tired for the long walk ahead. As the whole camp seemed to be asleep, I came back to see if Lin-nam would not drive me to my tent. He is often up late, for that is when he has the time to teach new tricks to his bears. But the Cathayan had just returned from some errand and was in no mood to hitch up his yaks again. I remembered seeing food set out here for one of you and so came to ask for help." He cut another slice of mutton. "Lin-nam was probably anxious for rest after all the excitement. You missed that incident. One of his bears went into a fury and threatened to get out of its cage." He looked up at Taikal. "But I am mistaken. This happened shortly after we met near the herds, and so you must have heard the disturbance."

Taikal made his tone careless. "Yes, I heard there was some commotion near the wagons." He wondered if Haroun had mentioned their meeting to the Cathayan. "Did Lin-nam tell you what the trouble was?"

"He thought someone had bumped the wagon in passing,"

the lute-singer replied, lifting the milk sack. "I did not join
the rush toward the noise, for Lin-nam sped away and left
his dancing bears. If the animals are not kept under control,
they can become excited, perhaps even dangerous. So I took
the Cathayan's place. The bears seemed to like my music,
for they danced until they were dizzy." He shook his head.
"You would think that in thanks Lin-nam would drive me
back to my tent. But perhaps he feared the bear would get
excited again." He loosened the horse's tether and easily
swung up on its bare back. "You shall have a song for this
favor, Taikal. Perhaps I will compose one about your
journey when the time comes for you to speak of it freely."
He waved in farewell.

Just before dawn the next morning Taikal awoke from
habit and long training. But nothing stirred in the camp, nor
did the expected cymbals clash. He went back to sleep.
When he awoke once more, the sun was well up, the camp
was stirring, and through the open entrance he could see
Yarkut starting the fire.

"We are starting at midmorning today," Yarkut said
when Taikal joined him at the fire. "The horses, and we,
too, need a good rest after yesterday's mud. We will make
up the lost time tomorrow."

The air was mild, and the earth, frozen during the cold
night, had thawed and was drying under the bright sun.
Everyone in sight was going around in deerskin shirts, many
of them bareheaded.

"This late start will give us time to decide what to do,"
Taikal said, as he prepared to boil some rice.

"There is more news," said Yarkut, deftly spearing pieces
of meat and arranging them over the flames. "The beishung

behind the drive line broke through last night and killed a horse."

"And I was on that horse," Taikal said.

Yarkut exclaimed his astonishment. "I wondered why you did not return after you went to the Cathayan's wagons! You were not hurt, were you, Taikal?"

He shook his head. "This is how it happened." Speaking softly, lest some passer-by overhear, Taikal told all that had passed since he had left Yarkut watching Lin-nam's bears.

"That was a very narrow escape you had, Taikal," marveled his friend. "Your horse must have been scented with the musk."

"If it were, I could not tell, for my nose was filled with the incense of Jiemdad's yurt. And I confess my wits were scrambled from the strong wine. For the same reason, the commander would not have noticed it either, and the servants would have no reason to question the scent."

"This seems to prove that Lin-nam is the guilty man, not Basukor," said Yarkut. "And my idea of Basukor slaying the beast which lived beyond the drive line is wrong. Yet where did he get the beishung pelt?"

"Perhaps the Tibetan adventurer delivered a pelt along with the three live animals he took to Kara Khitai," Taikal suggested. "Basukor could have made Lin-nam an innocent party to his scheme of killing our generals by using a trained beishung. I remember meeting the Cathayan the night I went to the left division camp to learn of the attack on Bayan. Lin-nam happened to mention that his second cage, the one with the 'fighting bears,' did not belong to him at all. He is merely paid to care for it."

"But surely he would soon discover that the 'bears' were

really beishungs!" Yarkut argued. "Basukor would not take that risk."

"Nor would Basukor take the risk of carting those beishungs around himself," countered Taikal. "But he could have invented some elaborate tale to fool Lin-nam. Perhaps the Cathayan has never seen those 'fighting bears' except in the dark, when they were covered with dye."

"But remember how the dye came off Haroun's boots when he but touched them with a damp palm," Yarkut objected. "Would not the dyed beishungs leave marks in the cage? Lin-nam would be sure to notice them when he cleaned the wagon."

Taikal shook his head. "The bottom of the cage would be littered from the animals. During Lin-nam's cleaning any dye marks would be washed away, and the Cathayan would never notice them. Besides, you said that he cleans that cage at night. But no matter, we will soon learn the truth when we challenge Lin-nam to uncover his third 'fighting bear.' And if he names Basukor as the owner, the magician will have a hard time explaining the beishung pelt he uses in his sorcery."

"I do not think Lin-nam will do as we ask unless we bring along someone in authority," Yarkut said. "Chepe Noyon seems to be in a better humor lately."

"He still rides by me without a word," Taikal said. "Jiemdad would be willing enough to come with us. He opposes Basukor and his magic and would be glad to prove that Beishung is a real animal."

"I still smart under Chepe Noyon's words that time we took him to the cave," said Yarkut. "I would like him to see that our suspicions are not campfire tales."

"Perhaps he will not be willing to come with us," said

Taikal. "But let us hope he will at least listen to our request."

After their meal they kicked dirt over the fire and sent a herder for their horses. Taikal replaced the red crest in his helmet before swinging into the saddle.

They found Chepe Noyon riding along the curving picket line, inspecting the right division's section. He favored his left arm, letting it rest across the pommel. He halted as they came up.

"I have heard the camp rumors, Taikal," he said. "And you need not think it makes a difference in my attitude. I know the Khan too well to believe he would send untried youths on important missions, though I have not tumbled your prestige by saying so."

"Neither Yarkut nor I started that talk, Chepe," Taikal answered.

"You have not vigorously denied the report either," the general retorted.

Taikal could feel his neck getting warm. "The purpose it serves is not that of increasing my prestige," he answered.

"A better purpose would have been served had you remained with the drive and endured the disgrace of breaking a hunt rule," Chepe returned. "Though the Khan gave you permission to leave for a while, do not think that he will forget your running away when it is time for you to become an officer."

Taikal turned his horse aside. "Come, Yarkut. We will get someone else to view the beishung."

"Just a moment!" Chepe ordered. He leaned forward in his saddle. "What do you have to do with Basukor and his tricks?"

Yarkut answered, "We do not mean Basukor's false

spirit, but a real animal, Chepe. There is one hidden in the camp, and we wanted to take you to it."

"A beast like the skin which Basukor exhibited?" the general asked. "A black and white animal such as Taikal slew? Very well, take me there. And let us hope the animal has not disappeared as had the mysterious cave markings you wanted me to see."

They rode across the camp to the wagons, then followed along until they found Lin-nam cleaning one of his cages.

"I have come to see your bears, Lin-nam," Chepe greeted the Cathayan. "I have heard amazing things about them."

Lin-nam jumped out of the cage and bowed before Chepe. "With pleasure shall I display them, honored general. My most profound apologies that the great Chepe Noyon must see me in such old garments, but I have been cleaning—"

Chepe waved impatiently. "It matters not. But hasten to bring your bears that I might examine them." He dismounted and handed his reins to Taikal.

The Cathayan walked to his other wagon nearby. "They are in here. Let me but roll up the curtains."

As Lin-nam entered the cage and began pulling up the felt cover, Yarkut flung a worried glance at Taikal. Within the barred wagon the two dancing bears drowsed contentedly.

"Would the honored general permit me to display my bears' tricks?" Lin-nam asked, prodding one with his foot.

"Do not trouble yourself," Chepe replied. "I have seen enough." His face, as he signaled Taikal to give him the reins, was filled with contempt for the two cadets.

Taikal said quickly, "Perhaps the general would like to see the fighting bear, Lin-nam. The one you keep in this cage that you were cleaning."

"That bear was sold last night," the Cathayan replied. "But if the honored general wishes to purchase a fighting bear of excellent quality—"

"Yes, tell us who bought the bear," Taikal urged. He hardly noticed that Chepe took the reins from his hands and mounted.

"Alas, I know not," replied the Cathayan. "All of the fighting bears belonged to someone else, and I was only paid to care for them. The owner arranged for their sale and delivery."

Out of the corner of his eyes Taikal could see that Yarkut had innocently brought up his horse to block Chepe from leaving. "When did Basukor put the bears in your charge?" Taikal asked, anxious to get to the heart of the matter before Chepe lost his temper.

"Basukor?" Lin-nam seemed puzzled. "My only business with Basukor was that he bought one of my dancing bears some time ago."

Chepe sighed with impatience. "Then who did own the fighting bears?"

The Cathayan shrugged. "There can be no harm in telling, now that all the bears are sold. They were owned by the commander Jiemdad."

"He lies!" Taikal exclaimed.

Yarkut leaned forward in his saddle. "Did Basukor pay you to say this?"

Fury struggled in the face of Lin-nam, but he quickly masked it with his usual Cathayan calm. "O, fortunate are the Mongols that they cannot commit insult!" Taikal flushed under the sarcasm. "And fortunate also," Lin-nam continued, "that the truth is easily discovered by asking the honorable Jiemdad." The Cathayan bowed low before Chepe Noyon. "Is there some other way in which I can serve the esteemed general?"

"Only that you remain and refresh my weary troops with your bears' tricks," Chepe replied. He turned his horse away and the cadets followed.

"Will you ask Jiemdad if he truly owned the bears?" Taikal asked as Chepe headed back into the camp.

"There is no need, for Lin-nam would not dare lie while he accepts Mongol hospitality," Chepe said. "Though I had not heard that Jiemdad had bears for sale, it is not uncommon for a person to be secretive about his goods. If the buyer thinks there is only one item for sale, he will willingly pay a higher price than if he knew the seller had several articles of the same kind."

"Then if Lin-nam had said all along that Jiemdad owned three fighting bears," said Taikal, "each bear would have brought a lower price."

"Except, perhaps, the last one," Chepe added. "Does this solve your mystery?"

"But what of the dye marks in the cave?"

"If dye it were, it was doubtless a tinted wash to improve the animals' coats," Chepe said. "It is a common practice." They had reached the picket line and Chepe seemed about to dismiss them.

"Chepe, will you not give us one more opportunity to show you that there is something wrong going on?" Taikal asked earnestly.

"I have no time for idle suspicions," the general said sharply. "Twice have I been taken to see nothing."

"But does that not prove someone is removing all traces

of his guilt?" Yarkut asked. "We had even found the man who sold this cheap black dye to Lin-nam."

"And to Basukor," added Taikal. "And one or two others. But the furrier suddenly left the drive only two or three days after we discovered this. It seems as if the guilty man paid him to go so he could continue his work unsuspected."

"Have you not examined the beishung pelt Basukor has?" asked Yarkut. "It bears marks of captivity and should prove that the black and white beasts were indeed trained to slay."

Chepe gestured impatiently. "You have mentioned both Basukor and Lin-nam. Which man are you accusing? Or do you seize upon any name that is convenient to explain your ideas? Lin-nam has conducted himself favorably all during the drive. As for Basukor and his magic, you must let the Khan deal with him."

"It is important to you, too, that we prove our suspicions," Taikal said boldly. "A trained animal does not come under the laws of the hunt, and so my saving you from one should cause you no embarrassment."

Chepe reflected briefly. "You must understand that I do not encourage you in this, for I do not credit your imaginary plot. Yet if you should discover some definite proof, I will listen gladly."

As they rode away, Yarkut asked, "Do you have some plan, Taikal, that you wish Chepe to witness?"

"No," Taikal admitted. "But I was certain he would not listen to us after today unless I made him promise. Perhaps we can think of something which would impress Chepe. There still remains the beishung pelt with its marks of captivity."

At their yurt, Yarkut began cleaning his boots of yesterday's mud while Taikal started to mend the weakened cinch of his saddle.

"It would seem that Basukor did indeed use the beast behind the drive line for his 'magic slaying' of Beishung," Taikal said. "Last night's attack was made by the beishung that had been hidden in Lin-nam's cart. Basukor's herder must have seen me arouse the animal with the scent. Then the spirit-talker knew he must at once release the animal and put an end to my investigations."

"Lin-nam also saw you near his carts last night," Yarkut pointed out. "I say he is the guilty one, and that ever since he joined the drive he has deceived Jiemdad. To my knowledge the commander has not had much interest in fighting bears and so could not judge their quality. Lin-nam could easily have persuaded him to buy a wagonload, then leave them in his care. Jiemdad would never know he actually owned three beishungs."

"But Lin-nam said Jiemdad arranged for their sale," Taikal protested.

"It would be easy for Lin-nam to send someone to Jiemdad to offer a high price for a bear. This 'buyer' could tell the commander that he preferred to move the bear himself, and thus Lin-nam could falsify the sale without entering into the bargain."

"And is this man of Lin-nam's the same one who followed us to Tibet?" asked Taikal.

"Perhaps. As for the third 'sale,' Lin-nam could have paid some innocent person to act as his agent."

"Lin-nam once told me that when his lad ran away at the beginning of the drive, he continued to get a little help from one or two friends he had made," Taikal recalled. "Could not these friends, or one of them, have been sent by Basukor?

Indeed, if there is a master of deceit among us, Basukor could easily have fooled both Lin-nam and Jiemdad. Perhaps it was he who in the beginning arranged for the appearance of cart and 'bears,' then made each man think the other was responsible for the animals."

"Taikal, you are making our task more difficult! If everyone connected with the 'fighting bears' has been fooled, where shall we pick up the strand to unwind the deceit?"

"It might help if we talked to the Cathayan's helpful friends," suggested Taikal. "Who is known to have been near Lin-nam and his wagons since the drive began?"

"It would have to be someone not afraid of handling large animals," Yarkut said.

The sudden strumming of a lute interrupted them. Haroun came from around their trail yurt and greeted them. "Yesterday ended on a happy note, though we did not hear of it until this morning," he said with a grin.

"We know not of what you speak," Yarkut replied.

"I had thought that surely the entire camp must know by now, what with Basukor driving his conjuring yurt up and down and bellowing curses at the top of his lungs," the singer said. "It seems that the effort of magically slaying Beishung has gone for little. Last night someone entered his yurt while he slept and stole the pelt of his favorite spirit."

"The beishung skin?" Taikal asked incredulously.

"It is gone?" Yarkut cried. It was their last clue.

"Gone!" Haroun laughed. "Without Basukor's permission, the weary god has returned home to rest from the incense and noisy chants."

So that was why Basukor and his servants were up when the entire camp slept! And no wonder the Tangut was rude and demanding. "But who could have stolen the beishung pelt?" Taikal asked. "Is anyone suspected?"

"No," said Haroun. "But the matter has been reported to the Master of Punishment, for even Basukor has a right to justice. No doubt the culprit will soon be found, and the pelt too."

"Unless it has been destroyed," said Taikal.

When Haroun had left, Yarkut said, "Then Basukor is not the guilty one, for he would not destroy the pelt which seemed to prove his tales of magic."

"He would destroy it gladly," replied Taikal, "rather than let it prove his guilt. Basukor, or actually his Tangut herder, saw me near Lin-nam's wagons. Then later that night the herder came up to me and saw that I had not been killed by the beishung."

"Others were up at the same time last night," Yarkut pointed out. "Lin-nam saw you. So did Kishlik, the lieutenant you told me about. And of course Haroun."

"But the pelt was stolen last night," Taikal objected. "And Lin-nam would not know until this morning that I was still alive." He thought for a moment, then shook his head. "Nor could Haroun have mentioned to Lin-nam my safe return, for when he left me, he rode to his own tent on a horse I loaned him. Just a moment!" He turned his mind back to the picket line, reliving every sight and sound. "Just before the beishung broke through the picket line, I heard the creak of wagon wheels."

"Lin-nam!"

"Basukor," Taikal said. "Or his Tangut herder."

"But you rode on," Yarkut said, "and found Basukor and his servants together."

"The cart could have been taken back to Lin-nam, who

then returned it to his customary place," Taikal insisted. "Haroun said that Lin-nam had just returned from some errand and was reluctant to hitch up the yaks once more. A fast horse, riding among the herds where the sound would be less noticed, could have taken the Tangut back to Basukor. And why was the magician up? Would the mere absence of his precious beishung pelt have awakened him?"

Yarkut gestured impatiently. "He heard a sound, or one of his servants did."

Taikal fastened the repaired cinch strap to his saddle, then began examining his bridle. "There is little sense in our discussing who is guilty, for now we have no means of proving that any attempts have been made against our generals."

"You still have the ivory vial of musk scent," reminded Yarkut. "Perhaps we could set a trap."

Taikal looked up. "Do you mean to have Lin-nam and Basukor in the drive line and have me accidentally spill the musk on them?"

"Something like that," Yarkut said. "Whichever one becomes frightened and runs off would be the guilty man."

"It would not prove anything at all." Taikal cut a worn strap from the bridle and began replacing it with a new piece of leather. "Our friend who shies not at murder would sit his horse until the beast came into view. And then no one would question a non-hunter if he galloped away. Besides, how can they ride with the drive line? Neither has the privilege."

"But we must do something, Taikal! The hunt festival is only a week away, and surely the murderer's plot will have succeeded by then. If we could only confront both men with a beishung and watch their reactions!"

Taikal gazed into the distance. "A beishung is coming

from Tibet," he said slowly. "But it is a wild creature, not trained to kill at the scent of musk."

They were silent for a while, fingers busy with their tasks, minds working furiously.

Yarkut said, "We, and the murderer, are the only ones here who know that the beishungs have been trained to kill. That is why no one else in the hunt suspects a plot. But if everyone were to see that the normal beishung does not kill humans—"

"The murderer would not let that happen," Taikal interrupted. "He would surely contrive to kill the gift from Tibet."

Suddenly they stared at each other.

"There is our trap!"

"If we but watched the wagon. . . !"

Excitedly they laid their plans. The biggest difficulty was that the Pandit Ch'en Po's gift beishung would not arrive for at least a week, perhaps longer. "And even to arrive then travel must be fast, using relays of animals," Yarkut pointed out. Yet it might be that the Tibetans had made excellent time and had then relaxed their pace, since they did not have to arrive until the hunt festival.

"They are certainly within our border," said Taikal. "We know our country better than they, and it might be that even if they are not farther advanced than they expected, we could show them trails that would hasten them."

The first step in laying their trap would be to ride out to meet the Tibetans. Then they must contrive to bring the Pandit Ch'en Po's gift into the camp before the hunt festival.

"The circle will soon be formed and the space between hunters will begin to close up," Yarkut said. "Soon units will start dropping out of the drive so the ring may be drawn tighter. Tomorrow or the day after I will ask Jiemdad to let my company be the first to retire. Then I can ride out to meet the Tibetans."

"You must make haste," Taikal advised. "The guilty man has withheld his hand so far, I think, because he knows we are suspicious. But the time grows short for the completion of his plan, and he may act before we can discover him."

Horsemen galloped through the camp, rattling on drums to announce the start of the day's drive. Taikal and Yarkut quickly struck the yurt and readied their belongings for the cart to pick up.

When Taikal galloped to the position of his new company, he was surprised to find Kishlik giving captain's orders. The lieutenant grinned when he saw Taikal. "I did not know until this morning that you are to take over this company," he said. "Now I have just learned that Pechen will not be back for some time."

"Pechen? Is this his company?"

"A curious turn of fortune, is it not?" Kishlik chuckled. "I well remember how quickly he set your standard aside when Jiemdad wished to lead his escort."

"But you were not in Pechen's company then," Taikal said. "Or you would have recognized him as a captain. In fact, for the first two weeks of the drive, you were in my company."

"I was attached to Pechen's unit later," Kishlik replied. "Now come and meet your other lieutenants."

Little ground was covered that day, but a great step was taken in the hunt. The extreme ends of right and left divisions had difficulty closing the circle, for the driven animals, sensing that their corridor to safety was threatened, began pouring through the gap. Chepe Noyon called for a hundred men to turn the animals back while the others closed the ring. Jiemdad sent Taikal's company.

When Taikal brought his unit up to the gap, he loosely arranged his men before the opening. Now the line drivers could concentrate on bringing the two ends together. It was a task of noise and confusion, of cymbals clashing and signal drums rattling, of warning cries and triumphant shouts. Horses whirled in every direction; padded lances swung hurriedly; blunt arrows whizzed through the air. One group of shield-bearers was working so hard that it went on foot and ran, crouching, toward the fleeing game.

There was no halt for the midday meal. Every man worked without pause, sweat streaming from each brow. Then, at last, with glad cries, right and left divisions met. The circle was closed!

The sun was setting, and there was only time for Taikal to lead his company back to its position in the line. The day's hunt was over and the picket horses were brought up.

"That was fine work, Taikal," Yarkut said as they ate the evening meal. "I heard that Chepe Noyon rode over to see how you handled your company."

"I saw nothing but horses and game today," Taikal said. "Tomorrow we close ranks, and then units will begin dropping out to tighten the ring."

"I have already asked Jiemdad to let my company drop out first," said Yarkut. "He seemed surprised that a student officer would be so willing to end his command. But he made no comment except to give me orders for the men."

"I had forgotten that the men who drop out of the drive

line would be set to work bringing supplies from Karakorum and making the fence for the ring," said Taikal.

"Jiemdad will not miss me as my men ride back and forth," Yarkut replied. "And Hirlan, with whom I ride, will understand that cadets have little interest once their work in the drive line is finished. He will no doubt issue the orders and think I am amusing myself riding around the countryside."

By the end of the next day the hunters had closed their ranks. Now they rode more slowly, flank to flank, each rider's stirrup touching that of his neighbor. Yarkut sent three squads out of the drive. "I will start with two less squads in the morning," he told Taikal that evening. "That means I must take out the other five units tomorrow. I wish I could set out to meet the Tibetans tonight."

"Can you arrange it so that Hirlan takes your place tomorrow?" Taikal asked. "Send five squads to Karakorum. They will think you are in the drive line, and the other five will think you are bringing back supplies for the festival."

"A fine idea. I will see Hirlan at once."

Yarkut was grinning when he came back. "It is arranged. Half of my company is at this moment grumbling because they must start a journey after a hard day's work. When they leave tonight, I will ride off so that anyone watching will think I have gone to give them additional instructions."

Later that evening fifty men rode off toward Karakorum, dried meat under their saddles and sacks of milk churning at the pommels. Yarkut prepared for his own journey, then bade Taikal farewell.

"Hurry," Taikal urged. "It makes me uneasy for you to be away, for that is one less pair of eyes to watch for trickery and two less hands to help overcome it."

During the next five days, while Yarkut was gone, Taikal

saw nothing to arouse further suspicion. Everyone in the drive settled down to the hard work of drawing the circle tighter. When the gap had been closed, the ring was eleven miles across. The drivers had halved the distance by closing up their ranks. Units continued to be taken out each day at various points of the circle, for the final hunt ring was to be only two miles in diameter.

Accidents occurred more frequently as the men rode in close quarters. Gone was much of the usual joking and laughter. The men muttered savagely as they slowly pressed forward, their horses stumbling on slippery rocks, flanks scraped from squeezing around trees, equipment and sometimes men being swept away as they crossed swift streams.

Basukor was doing a brisk trade, selling charms and false words. Many of the warriors who traded with him became apathetic, merely riding along in the drive and doing nothing to prevent accidents. Others became surly and began ignoring orders.

Jiemdad issued another announcement. Any warrior who carried Basukor's little felt idols was to be barred from entering the hunt ring. For the next day, at least, his regiment had fewer accidents.

The withdrawn units were kept hard at work carrying supplies from Karakorum. Often families returned with them, driving their cart-mounted household yurts to the hunting area. Trees were felled, and saplings were woven. Though picket horses often formed the hunt ring, this time there was to be a solidly built corral.

The families which joined the hunters began visiting Basukor. Jiemdad grew increasingly short-tempered as the household yurts displayed cloth idols and feathered charms, but his men only shrugged. How could they keep their wives from buying amulets? Women were easily amused with foolish things.

One crisp cold day shouting messengers went galloping along the circle. The drive stopped as if it had struck a wall. The men in Taikal's company speculated wildly.

Jiemdad galloped past, entering the woods at Taikal's left. The cadet captain turned his horse out of line and followed, twisting and turning between the trees.

He came to a clearing which sloped back into a valley that had been crossed not long ago. Dismounted warriors, some holding the horses in the line, talked excitedly. Many of the faces showed fear, and some sought comfort from the forbidden amulets hidden in their jackets. Riding up to the close-ranked horses, Taikal saw that Jiemdad was just inside the circle, examining the remains of an animal.

A few patches of fur lay here and there near the skeleton. From these and the shape of the skull, Taikal realized with a start that he was gazing at what was left of a giant panda, a beishung.

A horseman galloped up from the valley. Glad cries from the warriors greeted him. "Here is Basukor! He will know what to do. Make way! Let him see the beast." Before the spirit-talker could dismount, Jiemdad angrily pushed through the drive line to meet him.

"You have no business coming this close to the drive," he told Basukor.

"It is my business if someone seeks to discredit me," Basukor returned haughtily. "I demand to see the carcass that has been found."

Jiemdad laughed. "I will tell you all you need know,

magician. The creature was once a black and white animal which you call your god, Beishung. It was slain and eaten by ordinary wolves." He turned to the waiting soldiers. "Do you not see how Basukor has fooled you? The black and white beast is a real animal, not a spirit, or it could not have been killed by other creatures."

Basukor raised a commanding hand. "Do not let trickery misguide you," he told the warriors. "You know that some days ago the precious skin of Beishung was stolen from my yurt. Now we learn that the thief was anxious to give lie to my words. The pelt was no doubt tied around the flayed carcass of a bear and dragged into the circle so that wolves might destroy it. And this shabby trick is supposed to prove that Beishung is merely an animal!"

"The bones are some weeks old," Jiemdad replied contemptuously. "The skull is differently shaped from a bear's." He gestured toward the remains that lay just within the circle. "You men may go and examine it. Let your own senses convince you that you have nothing to fear. But do not let Basukor near, or you will soon be buying slivers of 'Beishung bone.' "

Someone rode along the drive line, dismounted, and slipped between the horses into the circle. But none of the warriors near Jiemdad attempted to follow.

The man who had gone to view the skeleton came back. It was Kishlik. "It is indeed an animal such as attacked the drive line."

"Go with Kishlik and see for yourselves," Jiemdad told his men.

The soldiers nudged one another, yet none dared approach the skeleton.

Jiemdad turned to Kishlik. "Gather up the remains and do not leave a scrap for Basukor. When we camp tonight, destroy everything completely."

Taikal spoke up. "May I assist the lieutenant?"

Jiemdad turned around in surprise. "Taikal! No, Kishlik can attend to the matter alone. Go back to your company." Then he added, "You have been doing fine work."

By the time Taikal returned to his place, he found that rumor had fled before him. The men were talking of the stolen pelt, tied to the carcass of a bear, and thrown to the wolves in order to discredit Basukor. Taikal wished that Yarkut would return quickly with the Tibetan beishung. Besides uncovering the murderer, the gift would show that the beishung was a real animal, not to be feared or revered as a spirit.

That evening, after supervising the picketing of horses for his company's section, Taikal found his trail yurt already set up in the camp. "Yarkut!" he cried.

"Come eat," said his friend, cutting meat into a bowl of rice. "I returned just an hour ago and have been stuffing myself ever since. I will be glad when the festival begins and we are rid of trail food."

Taikal joined him in the meal. "I feared you would not return in time. Tomorrow is the last day of the drive, and the festival begins as soon as the corral is built. Did you bring the Tibetans with you?"

"I have already helped them set up their tent near the wagon which carries the beishung. Even now there is talk in the camp of the marvelous black and white animal the Pandit Ch'en Po has sent to Genghis Khan."

"Have many people seen the animal yet?"

Yarkut grinned. "Oh no! It is to be kept as a surprise

when the festival begins. The Tibetans have already notified the Khan of this arrangement, and he has agreed." Then he leaned forward, lowering his voice. "In truth, Taikal, the beishung is not here. There is but a bear in the wagon, although that is even better. The guilty man may succeed in killing the Pandit's gift when he comes to the wagon tonight to keep his own beishung's training a secret."

"Where is the real beishung?" Taikal asked. "Has something happened to it on the journey?"

"No, but it will not arrive until three days from now, after the first day of the festival. The Tibetans had made all the speed they could, carrying the beishung in a cage slung between two horses and then in a wagon they purchased on entering the Nan Shan. Yet our trap must be set before the ring is opened to hunting, so I thought to use some substitute.

"On my way to meet the Tibetans, I had passed a Tatar traveling with a young fighting bear. Taking half of the beishung's escort with me, I returned and persuaded the fellow to let me bring his bear along for the festival. He is following more slowly, for his real purpose in traveling is to find an errant brother.

"I can not recall how I explained this to the Tibetans, but they seemed to feel that any arrangements I made were satisfactory. They probably think I have them following some Mongol custom!"

"That was quick thinking, Yarkut," Taikal congratulated him. He then described the finding of the beishung remains that day. "The skeleton was some weeks old, though I did not have an opportunity to examine it myself. This means that the animal, skin and all, was killed by wolves before Basukor's pelt was stolen. So the skin the spirit-talker had must have come from Kara Khitai, with the three beasts."

"Perhaps," Yarkut said. "But I think Lin-nam secretly sold it to him when he found no place for it in his plot. Has the beishung which attacked you been seen?"

"Not yet," Taikal said. "It will certainly show itself when the ring is opened to hunting. Then, sharp weapons or not, each general must alone face a maddened creature!"

"There is only tonight and two more nights in which to catch the murderer," Yarkut said. "We must be certain that everyone hears of the black and white animal from Tibet. That is a lot of work for us."

"And too obvious as a trap if we went around talking of it," Taikal pointed out. "But a lute-singer goes from fire to fire."

"Haroun's song of the beishung!"

"With the arrival of the Pandit's gift, it would be natural for him to sing such a song," Taikal said. "He could have learned it from the Tibetans."

Within an hour Haroun was strolling among the trail yurts and the mounted household dwellings.

"On thickly wooded slopes a strange beast dwells,
Men know not its name, though many names they say...."

It did not take long for Basukor to gather a crowd before the platform of his yurt. He took phrases of the song and cunningly twisted them into proof that Beishung was a spirit.

Jiemdad, face dark with anger, paced his horse among the yurts of his regiment, looking for charms dangling in doorways.

Chepe Noyon gave Taikal and Yarkut a nod of recognition when he saw them at a wrestling match.

Where the wagons and carts were drawn up, the Tibetans rested from their journey in a tent next to the felt-curtained cage they had brought. Nearby Lin-nam took out his dancing bears and began driving them toward an idle place among the fires.

Kishlik rode back to the camp after having secretly disposed of the beishung remains in the hills. When he returned, Haroun was still singing.

> *"White the body as fresh bone,*
> *Black the legs as lava stone. . . ."*

The night spun on in music and singing, in juggling and wrestling, in shadow puppets jesting, and bears dancing and fighting. Occasionally a bitter quarrel broke out, and there were accusations of using magic spells.

At last the fires began going out. The lute strings were loosened, the drums hung away. The bears and dogs and monkeys went back to their cages. The last drinking horn was set down, and yurt flaps dropped into place.

The moon was hidden by clouds that occasionally let light fall through. Taikal and Chepe Noyon slipped among the yurts toward the carts which encircled the camp. As they drew near the tent of the Tibetans, a shadow stepped out to stop them. It was Yarkut.

"We can not hide near the Tibetans' wagon," he muttered. "The Kashgai moved his cart full of dogs close to it. I crept away when I thought the animals were asleep, but they woke up and began growling. If we all go there now, they will bark until someone discovers us."

Chepe grunted. Taikal said, "Have you found another place for us?"

"Three separate places, a short distance from the Tibetans. The dog cage is on the fourth side. But one of us is certain to see whoever comes."

He led them to their stations, then went to his own. Taikal lay under a supply wagon. Looking out past two camel carts and a wagonload of fence poles, he could see the half-hidden cage that was supposed to contain the Pandit Ch'en Po's beishung. By shifting his position slightly, he could view the other half of the cage.

From the moonlight which intermittently fell through the clouds, Taikal knew that only an hour had passed in waiting. Yet it seemed much longer.

And then a shadow moved!

Taikal smothered an exclamation of disgust as the clouds closed up again. He heard a faint creak as of the bear moving inside its cage. Then came the throaty growling of half-wakened dogs. There was a flurry of footsteps. The moon came out from behind the clouds, and Taikal found himself gazing at the cage, a fold in the curtain showing where it had been disturbed.

Quickly he scrambled out from under the wagon, his sounds covered by the barking of dogs. He ran between carts, hoping his direction would intercept the fleeing man's. If only the moonlight would hold!

At the edge of the line of wagons he stopped. A man walked toward the first yurts of the camp, the moonlight strong on his face for one revealing instant before the clouds again brought back the dark.

Chepe and Yarkut found Taikal still gazing in stunned disbelief.

"Did you see who it was, Taikal?" Chepe asked, raising his voice above the barking. "Yarkut and I saw only shadows.

Had it not clouded over, one of us could have pursued him."

"Was it Lin-nam or Basukor?" Yarkut demanded impatiently.

"Neither," Taikal said, astonishment in his voice. "It was Jiemdad."

At dawn, three days later, Taikal sprang from his blankets as cymbals clashed and were answered by a roar of drums echoing through the great camp. The hunt festival had begun!

Yet Taikal's heart was heavy, for he was thinking over the plan he and Yarkut had formed that night Jiemdad had walked out of the shadows.

At first Chepe Noyon had insisted that Taikal had lost the real intruder and had mistaken Jiemdad for him. The commander could have been coming in from the herds, either after examining an injured horse or returning from a visit. Jiemdad was walking, while the guilty man surely would be running after starting up the dogs.

The Kashgai finally got up to quiet his dogs as the three walked to the tent of the Tibetans to see if by chance one of them had awakened and seen the face of the intruder.

They found the Tibetans clustered around the cage of the young fighting bear, gesturing and whispering excitedly. Yarkut talked to them and then explained to Chepe and Taikal. "The bear is dying," he said. "The Tibetans found fresh apricot stones and a half-eaten peach in the cage."

"Poison," Taikal said quietly.

Chepe chewed his lip thoughtfully. "I wish no word of this to be said. Can you arrange that, Yarkut?"

In the moonlight Yarkut nodded. "I will have them bury the animal secretly. Taikal and I will pay the Tatar when he comes for his bear. The Tibetans did not see anyone near the wagon."

"I also want you and Taikal to forget this entire matter," said Chepe. "You are mistaken when you claim someone has trained beishungs to attack the line. Tonight's incident is easily explained. Everyone knows how Jiemdad has been fighting Basukor's influence. He had the beishung remains destroyed so the magician could not use them to increase his hold on the men. Perhaps he feared that Basukor would contrive to get possession of the Khan's gift, if only to replace the pelt that was stolen from him."

"And is it not a serious matter to slay the Khan's gift?" Taikal asked. "Should this not be brought to his notice?"

"It was a foolish and dangerous thing for Jiemdad to do," Chepe replied. "In many ways Jiemdad has not displayed his leadership in a straightforward manner. Yet he has had a difficult time this summer, and he fears the loss of his men's loyalty, first through the humiliation of his capture, and now through Basukor's corrupting influence. He has acted in the only way he knows. His manner will change by next summer when he again feels secure in his position. Meanwhile I do not wish further trouble for him, as we have need of good warriors."

Later, in their trail yurt, Yarkut suggested, "We could bring Chepe along tomorrow night. Surely Jiemdad will come again when he hears no word of the animal's death."

"Chepe would not come," Taikal replied. "And if he did, and saw Jiemdad again, it would not change his mind. Besides, I think our commander is too fearful to expose himself once more."

"But surely when Chepe Noyon, Bayan, and Subotai take their turns in the hunt ring, they will carry with them the scent that will bring their deaths!"

"And when the commanders enter," Taikal said gloomily, "Jiemdad will ride his favorite roan stallion into the ring and slay a beishung that is by then well-fed and peaceful." Suddenly he struck his knee. "The roan! Yarkut, that is the only way."

They began laying a daring, desperate plan.

Now as Taikal dressed in the chill dawn, he thought over the drama that would unfold within an hour when the ring was opened to hunting.

Yarkut sat up, yawning. "You were asleep when I returned from my errand last night. Did you make the arrangement?"

"Yes. And did you do your part?"

Yarkut nodded as he reached for his boots. "It was easy. Give it to me now, before both of us forget and it is too late."

Taikal handed him a small cylinder and then strapped on his lacquered leather armor. As he reached for his sword, he noticed Jiemdad's gifts of sword and bridle gleaming in the dawn light that seeped through a crack in the yurt wall. He pointed to them. "The Tatar may have these in payment for his lost animal."

They went out into the crisp air to start the breakfast fire. The camp was already alive with excitement. Smoke curled up from the great household yurts whose numbers had increased as families had driven out yesterday from Karakorum. Servants hurried on their tasks; laughing children ran between wagons and dwellings, and warriors paced on their sleek horses, tall and proud in their leather armor. In the dawn breeze, colored streamers flapped from yurt doorways, from spears thrust into the ground, from the necks of barking dogs, and from the harness of passing horses. Women were dressed in their gayest garments, coiled hair sparkling with golden rings and ropes of pearls. Some of the household yurts had been moved from their giant carts to be pitched on the ground, for the festival was to last several days. In the air hung a rich golden-brown smell; the women had already started baking the many cakes and pastries that would be needed.

After a leisurely and lavish breakfast of meat, fish, cakes, and fresh fruit, the crash of cymbals rang through the camp. "The hunt begins," Taikal said. "I hope our plan goes well."

Yarkut kicked dirt over the fire. "I will see you at the ring."

They quickly saddled the horses Yarkut had brought up to the yurt the night before, and with a nod, went their separate ways.

Taikal trotted through the crowded camp until he came to the corral fence that had been thrown up yesterday under thousands of hands. He followed it, galloping over the clear ground, making for a high hill in the distance.

On the way he passed groups of friends and families who had ridden out earlier to claim a good place from which to watch. But there were few people at the top of the hill, where the Khan's white pavilion sat like a cloud. From there, when he arrived with his generals, Genghis Khan would observe the skill and courage of the men in the ring.

Taikal stationed his horse at one side of the great white tent, almost in front of the corral gate. As he sat waiting, others arrived and took choice positions. Haroun trotted past and waved a lazy salute.

The hill where Taikal sat his horse was the highest in the area, almost a mountain, and it offered a clear view of the hunting arena that was two miles in diameter. The lower hills, clear of trees and topped by the corral fence, circled a bowl-shaped valley. A sparkling stream leaped from the west side, where the hills broke off in steep cliffs. It plunged down, cutting a lazy pattern between the foot of the hills, around dense woods and patches of bushes, flowing across open meadow, here and there parting around a rise and meeting again, boiling through rapids when other streams swelled its waters and cut a deeper bed. In several places the waters had flooded into pools where the streams met steep hollows or were blocked by beaver dams.

The arena was crowded with game. With no place to flee, herds of gazelles and deer only continued browsing as three wolves flashed out of nearby woods and pulled down one of their number. A fox stormed a covey of quail, caught one, and settled down to eat while the others came to rest not far away. In a distant wood Taikal caught the flash of a leopard leaping upon a boar, while a startled black bear lumbered away. Two lynx, hunting together, crept through the tall grass toward a stream where a colony of beavers was fishing. Behind, a tiger patiently stalked them. A weasel raced after a hare, and Taikal began noticing the smaller game, the sables, ground squirrels, chipmunks, and marmots, which would be food for the others until the hunters came.

Saddle drums snarled commandingly. The crowd near

the pavilion parted. The Khan paced through on a white horse, a white yak tail streaming from his helmet, the two red feathers beside it almost matching the long red hair that fell to a tangle where his beard began. Bayan followed, resplendent in his red lacquered breastplates. And then came Subotai on a horse with gilded hoofs, followed by a magnificent Chepe Noyon in steel-plate armor. As each of the generals passed, Taikal was aware of the scent that meant death—the aroma of musk.

The Khan and his generals dismounted to take their places on embroidered silk cushions within the pavilion. A little later, as people continued to cluster along the hilltops, a much larger group of horsemen came to the pavilion. These were the commanders, but as they took their places behind the generals, Taikal saw that Jiemdad was not among them. He bit his lip worriedly.

He saw Chepe Noyon lean toward Bayan. "Where is Jiemdad?" But Bayan only shrugged.

Then Taikal noticed that each general wore on a golden chain around his neck a tiny ball woven of gold wire. Often these globes were stuffed with herbs to prevent illness, but sometimes they were filled with scented sheep's wool and given as luck gifts, for such presents were customary during festivals. Taikal knew what scent they carried now.

At last Jiemdad rode up on a gray mare, his face as angry as it had been the night he was looking for amulets among his troops.

"What kept you, laggard?" Chepe Noyon roared cheerfully as Jiemdad entered the pavilion.

Jiemdad bowed to the Khan. "I beg forgiveness for being late, O Khan. But my herder allowed my roan stallion to

wander off, and he is still trying to find it. That is the mount
I intend to ride into the ring."

"Let me replace your sorry news with happier," replied
the Khan. "According to our custom, you are to enter the
ring with the other commanders after the generals have
each had his turn. But I have chosen to make an exception
this year. After I have hunted, you may enter the ring
alone."

Jiemdad's face glowed with pleasure. He bowed very
deeply. "I hardly know how I can thank the Khan for this
honor, for surely I have not earned it."

"You are a true and faithful commander," the Khan replied. "I wish all men in the camp to see that I value such
men and that even the misfortune of war will not lessen them
in my eyes."

With another bow Jiemdad covered his embarrassed flush
at the reminder of his captivity that summer.

Taikal slipped out of his saddle and wrapped the reins
around a fence post. Then he forced his way through the
swollen crowd to where the officers' horses were kept behind
the Khan's pavilion, tied in pairs so they would not wander.
He loosened Jiemdad's gray mare, leading it to a herdboy.
"Take this horse back to Jiemdad's yurt, for he will ride
another."

He returned to his own horse just as the Hunt Master, in
his blue cloak embroidered with a golden bow and arrow,
raised a long curving yak horn and blew the signal. The notes
lingered in the hills. The crowd pressing against the corral
grew still.

Genghis Khan mounted his white stallion, then reached
for his bow. A dozen war-tipped arrows showed from the

quiver at his right hip. The wooden gate in front of the pavilion was opened, and the Khan trotted through, going down the great slope to the bottom of the valley.

Taikal could see the white horse plainly as the Khan galloped around the valley, choosing his prey. He ignored the deer and gazelles, paid no attention to fox or fluttering game birds. Then suddenly he wheeled his horse to meet a boar charging from a wood. Sun flashed on his streaking arrow as it hit, and the boar rolled on the ground.

Now the game sensed a newer, more deadly danger from the hand of man. Bushes parted; tall grass moved; things were slinking in the dark woods. Throaty snarls began drifting up from the hunt ring.

The Khan splashed across a stream and entered a woods. Soon a roar echoed from the trees. A horse whinnied. Then a long-haired leopard burst from the woods, staggered, and turned to face his enemy, an arrow sticking from its side. The Khan rode out, and as the leopard made a last desperate leap, the fatal arrow spun to its mark.

Then at the far end of the arena a cry arose. "Beishung! Beishung!" Taikal strained to see beyond the distant trees and was rewarded with a flash of white that was the bei-shung's mark.

The Khan had seen it, too, and galloped to meet it. He rode out of sight behind a wood.

After a while the Khan trotted out into a distant field. Suddenly he whirled his horse to meet a wolf pack racing toward him. He reared his mount against the snarling beasts, loosing arrows so quickly that Taikal could only catch their gleam as they spun in the sunlight.

As the Khan rode toward the pavilion side of the arena

to the shouted congratulations of the crowd, Taikal saw the beishung moving in some trees. It was still alive!

"Well done!" cried Chepe Noyon when the Khan joined them in the pavilion. "I am glad you saved the black and white beast for me. Jiemdad, you must not slay it!"

"I could not make the animal charge," the Khan said, puzzled.

Jiemdad leaned toward the Khan. "My herder has not yet come. Permit me to wait, that I may ride my favorite mount."

But just then Yarkut forced his horse through the crowd around the pavilion. He was leading Jiemdad's roan.

"Ah, my roan!" Jiemdad cried in pleasure. "But where is my herder?"

Yarkut handed him the reins. "He was fearful because he had lost the horse. Even when I brought the roan to him, he was afraid to take it to you and face your anger again. Is this the saddle you wanted?"

"It will serve," Jiemdad replied. "You have my thanks, Yarkut." He placed his foot in the stirrup, then paused, a look of utter disbelief on his face. "What is this odor?" He whirled, his face white. "What have you done?"

Yarkut shrugged. "Do not blame your herder if the horse has broken into a perfume merchant's stall."

Jiemdad backed away from his horse. "No, no. I will not ride."

Chepe sniffed the air. "It is the same scent as that contained in this talisman you gave me, Jiemdad. And in Subotai's and Bayan's. Does the gift which honors us insult you?"

Jiemdad turned to a guard. "Bring me my gray mare."

Taikal moved his horse to the edge of the pavilion. "I fear the gray has been taken back to your yurt, Jiemdad. You must ride the roan."

"What trickery have you worked?" Jiemdad cried.

"Do not hold up the hunt!" the Khan exclaimed. "You have before you the horse you were so anxious to ride."

The commander drew himself up before the Khan, controlling the panic in his voice. "I beg to be excused from the hunt, O Khan, because of illness. Indeed, I have not felt well for some time."

"Does the black and white beast frighten you?" Bayan asked with cold contempt. "Keep to the near side of the arena, and perhaps it will not charge."

"I fear it not." But Jiemdad's voice trembled.

"You will not lightly set aside the honor I have given you," said the Khan, his gray eyes hard with anger. "Mount your roan, and enter the ring at once!"

Jiemdad hesitated, then mounted and held out his hand for a battle spear. He trotted to the gate as the guards pulled it open. At a blast from the Hunt Master's horn, Jiemdad went down the steep slope into the arena.

The Khan glanced at Taikal, inquiry in his eyes. Taikal moved his horse close to the open gate. Yarkut leaned on the fence nearby.

Jiemdad stopped when he reached the bottom of the slope, his spear poised, head turning anxiously in every direction. He started up again, keeping to the clear places, avoiding the dense woods, the shadowed hollows, and the rushing streams where footing was insecure. A gazelle started up, and he did not give pursuit. A tiger crouched in the shadows, but Jiemdad gave it no heed.

Suddenly a black and white streak blurred through a patch of woods. Then the beast was out in open field, racing with incredible speed and fury toward the lone horseman.

Jiemdad jerked his reins when he saw the animal. His mount reared and slewed around. The battle spear was shaken from Jiemdad's grasp. Frantically he tugged at the hilt of his sword.

The crowd was screaming now. Someone climbed the fence and swayed there, his voice heard in spite of the noise. "Beishung! Beishung, you have returned!" It was Basukor.

Jiemdad shot his half-drawn sword back into the scabbard, and his heels beat against his stallion's sides. He galloped toward the pavilion side of the arena, the black and white animal streaking in pursuit, rapidly closing the great distance between beast and prey.

When Jiemdad reached the slope leading to the corral gate, Taikal maneuvered his horse to block the opening. The beishung was close to the hill as Jiemdad stormed up the slope. The roan stallion reared as it met with Taikal's mount.

"Let me through!" Jiemdad cried, jerking his plunging mount's head furiously.

"First tell the truth!" Taikal shouted, bracing himself in the saddle as his horse tried to prance out of the way.

Jiemdad glanced down at the beast which had just reached the bottom of the hill and was starting up.

"It will kill me!" he cried.

"Confess you are a traitor," Taikal demanded.

"Yes, yes!" Jiemdad cried, the roar of the beishung growing louder. "I made a bargain with Gutchluk!"

Taikal wheeled his horse out of the way. Jiemdad plunged through. The wooden gate slammed shut.

"How did you arrange the trap that caused Jiemdad to confess?" Haroun asked as they sat around the evening fire.

"I remembered something he told me," said Taikal. "And also something that Chepe Noyon had said."

The great circular camp was lively with light and laughter, music and merrymaking. Trained animals performed their tricks; the shadow play acted its comedy; wrestlers grunted, and jugglers tossed their colorful balls. Pheasant, venison, rabbit, and other meats sizzled over the fires, and servingmen went through the crowds with great platters of fruits, nuts, and pastries. Drinking horn vied with horn in mutual congratulation. Hundreds of men were still at work, salting down the remaining game animals that had been taken from the arena that day. Women worked in chattering groups as they scraped the hides and furs they would make into clothing for the coming winter.

Haroun had come to slake his thirst and hear the entire story of Jiemdad's treason.

"Jiemdad had told Taikal he planned to ride his favorite roan into the ring," Yarkut explained. "So late last night I hid the roan. When the hunt was about to begin, I brought the roan to Jiemdad after applying the scent Taikal had brought from Tibet."

"The same night Yarkut took Jiemdad's horse, I went to the Khan," Taikal said. "I persuaded him to let Jiemdad enter the ring before the generals, to show the commander's men that the Khan still respected him in spite of his having been captured by the enemy. Chepe Noyon had given me my argument when he said that Jiemdad's disposition would improve when he felt more secure in his command. I was certain that the Khan would feel the same way."

"Everything depended on Jiemdad being the first to face the beishung," Yarkut said. "We realized that he would contrive to have each general bear the scent which would make the trained animal charge viciously. The plot had to be exposed before they took their turns in the hunt ring."

"We did think that Jiemdad would confess the meaning of the scent before he entered the arena," Taikal said. "But when he went in, I had to block the way out, because I realized that nothing short of death itself would make him reveal the truth."

Haroun swept a cord from his lute. "A fine scene for a song! But I wish I might have been present when the Khan held his conference in the pavilion."

"Then you would have missed seeing the beishung killed," Taikal said.

After Genghis Khan had learned the cause of the beishung's charge, he had sent the Hunt Master and his men into the arena to slay the beast, thus showing thousands of people that the animal was not covered by the rules of the hunt.

That long discussion within the pavilion had gone on while twenty-nine commanders entered the ring, followed by the other groups of officers, according to rank. The cadets had been the last group to enter the arena, for the troops would take their turn during the next two days.

Taikal glanced at his spear thrust into the ground, two wolf tails and four gazelle tufts fastened to it. Yarkut's spear bore the tails of a lynx, three foxes, and a deer. Between the spears lay a bear's head, for they had slain it together.

"What made Jiemdad turn traitor?" Haroun asked.

"It started long ago at a battle in the Duntulun Shan," Taikal said. "Jiemdad and his brother both fought there, but Jiemdad hung back while his brother struck boldly. When the Khan honored the brother above him, Jiemdad was bitten with jealousy. It was a long time before he overcame his timidity and won a higher rank. By then his brother was dead, but envy had become a part of Jiemdad's character, and a hero's reward did not satisfy him. He wanted to rule an empire of his own."

"But there was nobody left to rule," Yarkut added. "Through the passing years Genghis Khan had absorbed all the small quarreling tribes into one vast, prosperous empire. Now Jiemdad's only hope of becoming a khan lay in betrayal. When Gutchluk marched in to take over Kara Khitai, Jiemdad thought him a man after his own heart, and he seized his chance when war broke out between Gutchluk and Genghis Khan."

"He allowed his regiment to be captured easily," Taikal said. "And demanded to be taken to Gutchluk at Gu-Balik, so that his regiment could not see him becoming friendly with the enemy."

"Why did I not guess?" Haroun exclaimed. "We did think it unusual for Gutchluk, the khan of Kara-Khitai, to send for any man beneath the rank of general. Had Bayan not rescued us, we might have become suspicious."

Gutchluk wanted Jiemdad to slay the Khan's principal generals, but Jiemdad was afraid to attack them directly. Then together they contrived the scheme of using the three beishungs that had been sent to Gutchluk the year before. The strange animals could do anything, and it would seem that it was part of their nature. Gutchluk had the three beasts trained through hunger and abuse to attack and kill at the scent of the Tibetan musk deer.

"But why musk from Tibet?" Haroun asked.

"The odor carries for a great distance," Yarkut explained.

"And the exact scent could not be duplicated in the camp and cause an unplanned charge."

The beishungs were hidden in a cave near the Karakhitaian border. When the hunt began, Jiemdad brought them up in their cage, then hired Lin-nam to care for them. He paid the Cathayan's lad to run away, then sent Pechen to become friendly with Lin-nam and help out with the "fighting bears."

"I often noticed Pechen near the cages when I would visit Lin-nam and help him with his dancing bears in exchange for songs," Haroun said.

Lin-nam never knew what was really in the cage. Every second or third night Pechen took the animals to a cave for "training" while the Cathayan cleaned their wagon. "Actually Pechen fed the animals during those times with food scented with musk," Taikal said. "Pechen, who aided Jiemdad's treachery, also bought a quantity of cheap dye from a Muscovite furrier at the beginning of the drive. The white bodies of the beishungs were kept colored black in the wagon. The disguise also helped Pechen in slipping an animal through the picket line. Then in some patch of woods or a cave he would wash away the coloring and let the animal loose for its attack. He told Lin-nam that Jiemdad had sold the animal."

The clumsy merchant who spilled musk scent on Chepe Noyon had been paid by Jiemdad, but he was told it was to be a joke. "Chepe ordered the merchant away from the drive, or we might have questioned him," Yarkut said. For the second attack, Jiemdad had sent Pechen with a cloak as a gift for Bayan. The musk odor was explained by saying that the garment had been packed in a box of spices to preserve it against insects.

When Taikal slew the beast which attacked Chepe Noyon, Jiemdad thought that he suspected enough about the plot to make him willing to break the most important hunt rule. He asked to have Taikal transferred to his regiment so he could watch him. To hide this real reason, he dwelt upon his dislike for the cadet. One of the ways he showed this was to have Pechen present Taikal with the beishung pelt as a "cloak." "If I had kept the skin," said Taikal, "I would have found the scars much sooner, and perhaps we would not have had to journey to Tibet." Later Jiemdad realized that the pelt would reveal the animal's captivity.

After the second beishung had killed the warrior who had thrust himself in front of Bayan, it remained ahead of the drive. Jiemdad attempted to keep the animal alive by loosing the picket horses and two or three dogs, for the beishung was trained not to feed without the scent. Then, fearful of discovery, he had finally let the beast starve. "Great hunger probably drove the beishung to go against its training and kill small game," Taikal said. "But before it could regain its strength, wolves attacked it."

Jiemdad soon found that humiliation did not keep Taikal from asking questions about the strange beast. Pechen told him that the cadet had questioned the Muscovite furrier. Jiemdad was relieved when the furrier suddenly decided to leave the drive.

From the man Taikal had placed in charge of his squad, Jiemdad learned of his departure. Pechen was sent to follow. "His orders were to discover our errand," said Yarkut. "And to slay us if we stumbled across the plot." But Pechen never returned.

"You were gone for three and a half weeks," Haroun said.

"Why did Jiemdad not try again to kill Bayan, Subotai, and Chepe Noyon?"

"He was too cautious," Yarkut explained. "Pechen had always done the actual work, but now he was on his way to Tibet. Jiemdad did continue to feed the third beishung, telling Lin-nam that this 'fighting bear' was too valuable to entrust to Pechen for training." Lin-nam had also been told in the beginning not to disclose ownership of the animals, for Jiemdad wished to give the impression that he had only one bear for sale. In this way he could get a higher price for each one. Lin-nam had no reason to question this, for it was a common device, frequently used.

"Jiemdad was also afraid that some other soldier might take a beishung attack upon himself, and the work would be for nothing," Taikal said. "He realized now he could not keep a beishung alive behind the drive line, and he had only one animal left. Neither could he contrive to scent all three generals at once during the drive without arousing suspicion. Then, too, Basukor began to build a false worship of the black and white animal. With everyone constantly thinking of the beishung, no attack would come as a surprise. That is why he set himself against Basukor."

"Now tell me how you found the scent," Haroun said.

Taking turns, they told him of their perilous journey, including the death of Pechen.

Their safe return startled Jiemdad. When Pechen did not come back after another three days, Jiemdad was convinced he had been slain by the cadets.

That evening, seeing Taikal going toward Lin-nam's wagons, he followed on his horse. When the beishung became aroused, Jiemdad realized that the cadets had come upon the secret of the musk scent. He decided they would have to die.

He insisted that Taikal come at once to his yurt. While waiting for the cadet to get a horse, Jiemdad took Lin-nam aside and instructed him to bring his wagon to a place near the picket line. The third "bear" had been sold and the new owner would take it away. The Cathayan was to come for his wagon a few hours later.

As an excuse for his sudden invitation, and to allay Taikal's suspicions, Jiemdad offered the cadet the command of a company and filled his arms with gifts. He excused himself during the evening and went out to take the beishung through the drive line and wash off the concealing dye. Utter desperation forced him to take Pechen's role, and he was fearful that the sentries might see him. Returning, he scented Taikal's horse, then re-entered his yurt to continue playing host.

The next morning Jiemdad had been shocked to find Taikal still alive. But, oddly enough, the cadet captain had not seemed to suspect him of the attempt on his life.

Now Jiemdad worked out his final plan. In nine days the generals would take their turns in the hunt ring. The beishung would stay alive for that time. Jiemdad would kill the generals with one stroke by giving each a gift bearing the deadly scent. Surely not even Taikal and Yarkut would notice the odor in the crowds and excitement of the hunt. The two cadets would later be disposed of in some way lest hindsight show them the truth that they had luckily missed so far.

"But suddenly a beishung arrived from Tibet!" Yarkut grinned. "Fearing that the normally shy animal would show

that the others must have been trained or goaded into unnatural attacks, Jiemdad went that night to poison the Khan's
gift. It was then we found who the murderer was. That night
we made our plans and trapped Jiemdad with his own
trick."

Haroun thoughtfully strummed his lute. "Why was
Genghis Khan never threatened by the beishungs? Surely,
if Gutchluk hoped to—"

"Gutchluk wanted to defeat Genghis Khan on the battlefield so that his reputation would be established and his
power greatly increased," Yarkut explained. "And if our
Khan were murdered, Gutchluk knew another one would
be elected. Fearing that a new khan would surprise, and perhaps defeat, the Karakhitaians with different battle tactics,
Gutchluk would not let Jiemdad attempt to slay Genghis
Khan."

"I know that Basukor was not part of Jiemdad's plot,"
Haroun said. "Yet how did he gain possession of the beishung
pelt?"

"Basukor confessed his trickery," Taikal said. "When I
threw Jiemdad's 'cloak' into the fire, Basukor immediately
snatched it from the flames. I saw that sudden movement,
but not knowing then who the man was, I thought only that
some angry warrior was starting toward me. Pechen and the
other men were too busy watching me to notice Basukor.
Only later Jiemdad realized how dangerous the pelt could
be as evidence against him. But both he and Pechen thought
the skin had been burned."

"Jiemdad was furious, and very frightened, when Basukor
later displayed the pelt," Yarkut added. "That was another
reason he hated the 'spirit-talker.' Pechen had left the camp

to follow us and did not return. So Jiemdad sent Kishlik to steal the pelt."

"I know not the man," Haroun said.

"He is a lieutenant, a good officer and a sensible man," Taikal replied. "Kishlik did not know Jiemdad's real reason for wanting the skin destroyed. But he agreed with him that Basukor's nonsense was dangerous for the army's morale and consented to steal the pelt. The night he chose to do this happened to be the same night that the beishung attacked me."

"Basukor performed his 'magic summoning of Beishung' with a dancing bear he had bought from Lin-nam," Yarkut explained. "He bleached the bear to make it resemble the beishung and used the same cheap dye Jiemdad had employed to disguise the animal while it was brought through the camp and hidden under the wagon. When the colored smoke was thick enough, the Tangut herder left off playing his flute and went beneath the cart. There he washed off the dye, and at Basukor's signal, he sent this 'beishung' into the open. When Basukor clapped his hands, the trained bear played dead. More smoke hid the Tangut as he took the bear back under the wagon and then rejoined the other servants on the platform. That night the bear, again dyed, was taken away to be slain and buried far behind the camp."

"But surely Basukor found the scars on the pelt!" Haroun exclaimed. "Did this not make him suspect trickery?"

"He realized there was a plot of some kind," Yarkut replied. "But to reveal it would also expose his own shamming. He hoped, too, that whoever was responsible would pay him for his silence. Jiemdad paled when he learned today that he could have made Basukor into an ally. Indeed, he might have thought of that had not Basukor frightened him badly by naming his 'spirit' Beishung."

"It was from Lin-nam that Basukor learned one of the names of the black and white beast," Taikal said. "When I slew the first animal, the Cathayan recalled from early childhood stories of the mysterious beishung. It happened that Basukor was the first to whom he mentioned these tales. The magician-to-be made him promise to keep it a secret. Later, when he built up his false worship, he threatened Lin-nam to keep him quiet about the name and the bear he had bought from him. Lin-nam mentioned the bear only once, when we practically accused him of trickery in front of Chepe Noyon."

"Lin-nam should have reported Basukor's threats," Haroun said.

"He was used to Gutchluk's ways with his subjects," Yarkut replied. "And he was frightened."

"What will happen to Jiemdad and to Basukor?" the singer asked.

"Usually traitors are executed," Yarkut said. "But the Khan decided it would be a greater punishment for Jiemdad to be sent to a distant tribe to perform the work of a servant. At sunset today Basukor started out of the empire under escort. His servants have already found better employment."

"And I will ride with Chepe Noyon in next summer's war against Kara Khitai," said Taikal with a grin.

A messenger reared his horse close to the fire and spoke swiftly. The cadets ran to their horses picketed nearby. "The real beishung is arriving, Haroun," Yarkut shouted as they swung into their saddles. "Genghis Khan has asked us to ride out with him."

They galloped recklessly to the edge of the camp where they found the Khan on his white horse, waiting with Chepe Noyon and those Tibetans already in the camp. The Khan signaled the cadets to ride on either side of him. They started toward a cluster of torches moving in the distance.

"Basukor is gone," said Genghis Khan. "And now the shadow he has laid upon my people will be swept away by truth."

They rode on to meet the caravan.

Bell, Sir Charles. *The Religion of Tibet*, Oxford University Press, London, 1931.

Boulenger, Edward G., and others. *Wild Life the World Over*, Wm. H. Wise and Co., New York, 1947.

Bretschneider, E., M. D., editor and translator. *Mediaeval Researches from Eastern Asiatic Sources; Fragments Towards the Knowledge of the Geography and History of Central and Western Asia from the Thirteenth to the Seventeenth Century*, 2 vols., K. Paul, Trench, Trübner and Co., London, 1888.

Curtin, Jeremiah. *The Mongols: A History*, Little, Brown and Co., Boston, 1908.

Drimmer, Frederick, editor. *The Animal Kingdom*, by George G. Goodwin [and others], 3 vols., Doubleday and Co., Garden City, New York, 1954.

Goodrich, L. C. *A Short History of the Chinese People*, 2nd edition, Harper and Bros., New York and London, 1943.

Harkness, Ruth. *The Lady and the Panda; an Adventure*, Carrick and Evans, Inc., New York, 1938.

Huc and Gabet. *Travels in Tartary, Thibet and China, 1844–1846*, Paul Pelliot edition, translated by William Hazlitt, 2 vols., George Routledge and Sons, London, no date. Originally published in 1852.

Komroff, Manuel, editor. *Contemporaries of Marco Polo, consisting of the travel records to the eastern parts of the world of William of Rubruck (1253-1255); the journey of John of Pian de Carpini (1245-1247); the journal of Friar Odoric (1318-1330); and the oriental travels of Rabbi Benjamin of Tudela (1160-1173);* Liveright Publishing Corp., New York, 1928.

Polo, Marco. *The Travels of Marco Polo*, Benedetto text, translated by Aldo Ricci, New York, The Viking Press, Inc., 1931.

Shen, Tsung-lien and Liu, Shêng-chi. *Tibet and the Tibetans*, Stanford University Press, Stanford, California, 1953.

Tate, George H. H. *Mammals of Eastern Asia*, The Macmillan Company, New York, 1947.